She wanted him.

She'd tried to deny it, but the wanting did not go away. So she was yielding to it, finally, her capitulation at last complete—so much so that she almost stopped in midstep and turned to him and…

No.

Not here. Not now.

Still, she simply couldn't resist turning back to Fletcher. "I am glad," she conceded. "That you kept after me. That it's worked out so well."

He took a long time to answer—sizzling, delicious seconds during which heat shimmered in their shared glance. "I'm pleased, too. Very much so," he said at last, and they both knew he referred to more than KinderWay.

Cleo leaned back against the open door and allowed it to happen—for one more sweet, seductive moment before he left her—to get lost in his beautiful, dangerous eyes.

Dear Reader,

No matter what the weather is like, I always feel like March 1st is the beginning of spring. So let's celebrate that just-around-the-corner thaw with, for starters, another of Christine Rimmer's beloved BRAVO FAMILY TIES books. In *The Bravo Family Way,* a secretive Las Vegas mogul decides he "wants" a beautiful preschool owner who's long left the glittering lights and late nights of Vegas behind. But she hadn't counted on the charms of Fletcher Bravo. No woman could resist him for long....

Victoria Pade's *The Baby Deal,* next up in our FAMILY BUSINESS continuity, features wayward son Jack Hanson finally agreeing to take a meeting with a client—only perhaps he got a little too friendly too fast? She's pregnant, and he's...well, he's not sure what he is, quite frankly. In Judy Duarte's *Call Me Cowboy,* a New York City girl is in desperate need of a detective with a working knowledge of Texas to locate the mother she's never known. Will she find everything she's looking for, courtesy of T. J. "Cowboy" Whittaker? In *She's the One,* Patricia Kay's conclusion to her CALLIE'S CORNER CAFÉ series, a woman who's always put her troublesome younger sister's needs before her own finds herself torn by her attraction to the handsome cop who's about to place said sister under arrest. Lois Faye Dyer's new miniseries, THE McCLOUDS OF MONTANA, which features two feuding families, opens with *Luke's Proposal.* In it, the daughter of one family is forced to work together with the son of the other— with very unexpected results! And in *A Bachelor at the Wedding* by Kate Little, a sophisticated Manhattan tycoon finds himself relying more and more on his Brooklyn-bred assistant (yeah, Brooklyn)— and not just for business.

So enjoy, and come back next month—the undisputed start of spring....

Gail

Please address questions and book requests to:
Silhouette Reader Service
U.S.: 3010 Walden Ave., P.O. Box 1325, Buffalo, NY 14269
Canadian: P.O. Box 609, Fort Erie, Ont. L2A 5X3

THE BRAVO
FAMILY WAY

CHRISTINE RIMMER

SPECIAL EDITION

Published by Silhouette Books

America's Publisher of Contemporary Romance

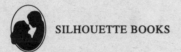 SILHOUETTE BOOKS

ISBN 0-373-24741-9

THE BRAVO FAMILY WAY

Copyright © 2006 by Christine Rimmer

Books by Christine Rimmer

CHRISTINE RIMMER

Christine is grateful not only for the joy she finds in writing, but for what waits when the day's work is through: a man she loves, who loves her right back, and the privilege of watching their children grow and change day to day. She lives with her family in Oklahoma. Visit Christine at her new home on the Web at www.christinerimmer.com.

For my son Matt and his new bride, Jenny.
May love, happiness and truth always be yours.

Chapter One

Fletcher Bravo rose from his sleek leather swivel chair. He braced his lean hands on his black slate desktop and canted toward Cleo Bliss. "I want you," he said. "Name your price."

A thoroughly unwelcome thrill shivered through Cleo. She had to remind herself not to shift nervously in the glove-soft guest chair.

Calm, she thought. *Serene. Under no circumstances can he be allowed to sense weakness.* She met those eerily compelling pale gray eyes of his with a level, no-nonsense stare.

I want you....

It was, Cleo told herself, only a figure of speech. He

didn't refer to Cleo specifically but to the top-quality service that Cleo and the people who worked for her could provide. If there was another, very sexual meaning in his words, Cleo chose not to acknowledge it—just as she chose not to recognize the hot little flares of excitement and attraction that had sizzled beneath her skin since she'd entered the CEO's corner office several minutes before.

Cleo already had a man in her life and he was nothing like the one across from her. Driven, powerful, dynamic men in gorgeous hand-tailored suits just weren't her style. She'd spent a good portion of her childhood watching what such men could do to the women they wanted.

Lesson learned. In spades.

She shouldn't even be here. She certainly didn't *want* to be here. But the man across from her had insisted. He'd started by having his associates approach her. Repeatedly. Each time she'd turned them down.

Fat lot of good declining had done. He'd called and said he wanted to meet with her personally. What could she do? In the past couple of years, Fletcher Bravo and his half brother, Aaron, had become major players in the gaming and megaresort world of Las Vegas. No smart businesswoman would offend either of them if she could help it.

So here she was. Meeting with him. Trying to get him to understand the word *no*.

So far she wasn't having a whole lot of success. She

cleared her throat and told him for what seemed like the hundredth time, "I'm sorry, but I'm just not prepared right now to take on a project of this magnitude."

Those wolfish eyes narrowed slightly. "Get prepared."

Cleo let a long beat of silence elapse before carefully suggesting, "Maybe I'm not making myself clear…."

"You are. As glass. But I'm not listening—and the day will come when you'll thank me for not listening. Because this is an opportunity you can't afford to pass up. This is growth, pure and simple. Growth that the Bravo Group will bankroll. Your facility here at Impresario will be double the size of what you've got at your current location. Inside and out, you'll get all the space you require. State-of-the-art equipment. Whatever you need. Say the word and it's yours."

"It's just not that simple."

"Oh, but it is."

"At KinderWay," she said patiently, "we're much more than a day-care service. We base our work on proven child-development techniques. For the program to be effective, it has to be consistent and ongoing. We're not set up for drop-ins."

"I realize that." He lowered his head and looked at her from under the dark shelf of his brow. "And you won't *be* a drop-in service. We plan to keep the regular day care for our guests. Employees with infants or workers who need day care only for after school can continue with our original program. I want KinderWay for the preschool kids only to start. And I want it exclusively for children of Bravo Group employees, both here at Impresario and at High Sierra."

High Sierra and Impresario were sister resort/casinos. They claimed a big chunk of prime real estate on opposite sides of the Strip and were connected by a glittering glass breezeway that crossed Las Vegas Boulevard five stories up. Both were owned and run by the Bravos. Fletcher was CEO of the newer Moulin Rouge-themed Impresario. Aaron Bravo, Fletcher's half brother, ran High Sierra.

Though Fletcher had yet to say so, Cleo knew the real reason he had decided he wanted the best preschool in Las Vegas on-site at Impresario. She could Google with the best of them, and in preparation for this meeting she'd done her homework. The photograph mounted in a brushed-chrome frame on Fletcher's polished-stone slab of a desk told the real story here and confirmed what Cleo already knew. The little girl in the picture had brown hair and big, solemn dark eyes.

Fletcher must have caught the direction of her gaze. "My daughter, Ashlyn. She'll be five in two weeks."

"Almost old enough for kindergarten," Cleo said gently. "She'll outgrow her need for a preschool in no time at all."

He shrugged. "I know that at KinderWay you take children up to first grade. So if you opened a facility here, Ashlyn would be at KinderWay for eighteen months—at least. And even longer if we can get you to extend your program through the third grade." He waited, as if for a comment from her. She gave none. He folded his tall frame back into his chair. "Ashlyn's nanny, Olivia, has been with her ever since Ashlyn's mother died and Ashlyn came to live with me. Unfortunately Olivia is leaving us, going back home to London."

None of which affected the decision Cleo had already made. "We have a two-year waiting list at KinderWay, but I'll see what I can do about—"

"Two years." He was shaking his dark head. "More proof that you need a plan for expansion. You're losing business, turning people away."

He was right. It had been four years since Cleo opened her preschool. Demand had grown much faster than she'd anticipated. She couldn't keep up with it. She regretted that. But she had no intention of overextending herself or her staff.

She told him, "Opening a KinderWay here at Impresario for your employees will do nothing to reduce the waiting list we already have."

"No. But it *will* provide a model for growth, get you moving in the right direction."

She thought, *How dare you presume to know the right direction for KinderWay?* She said with great care, "You don't understand."

"*I* think I do."

"The *quality* of the care we provide is what matters. The last thing I want is growth for its own sake—and you have to have thousands of employees here. Which means we're talking about a *lot* of children. I can't see how we can possibly accommodate—"

"You're right. Here and at High Sierra combined,

we employ over five thousand people. And those thousands have hundreds of children of preschool age. Many of those children are already in satisfactory care situations. And in any case, not all of them could be included—at least, not at first. So this would be a flagship program. We'll see how it goes, then build on it."

"A bold experiment. And expensive."

He nodded, a regal dip of his dark head. "Employees who use the service will pay for it—below cost, which should make it affordable for them. I'm projecting that the expense to the Bravo Group will be recouped in increased worker productivity."

And *she* projected that his interest in the program would fade as soon as his daughter grew old enough to move on. "Fletcher, I don't know any other way to say it. I already have my hands full with—"

"Wait." He spoke softly, but it was clearly a command.

And how many times had he interrupted her so far? She'd lost count. Tension gathered between her shoulder blades. She ordered it away. Folding her hands in her lap, she waited. Calmly.

Serenely.

Fletcher, meanwhile, had turned his attention to his state-of-the-art flat-panel computer screen. He began click-clicking with his cordless mouse.

As instructed, Cleo waited, watching him, her gaze taking in his wide, powerful shoulders, his strong, tanned throat, the handsome cleft in his square chin, the tempting, full shape of his sensual mouth, the…

Cleo caught herself.

Staring at Fletcher Bravo—bad idea.

She looked past him, out the wall of windows behind him, at the bold, smog-layered sprawl of Las Vegas and the bare humps of the mountains, hazy in the distance. Above the city, the January sky was overcast, an unbroken expanse of gunmetal gray. She ordered her mind to pleasant thoughts: a rainbow forming in a waterfall; the laughter of children; the bright, cheerful room at KinderWay where the youngest students learned and played...

"Come here," Fletcher said.

She refocused on him, meeting again the paler-than-gray eyes that were somehow sharper than any man's eyes had a right to be—and hadn't she read somewhere that his father, the notorious murderer and kidnapper, Blake Bravo, had had pale, wolflike eyes? "Excuse me?"

A corner of Fletcher's sexy mouth lifted in a hint of a smile. "I said, come on over her. I want you to see this."

Why? There was simply no point. Whatever he had on that big screen of his wouldn't change a thing. Why did he refuse to understand that she'd made her decision on this matter? Why couldn't he accept that she was only here as a courtesy, to let him know in person that she would not be accepting his offer?

As she tried to come up with a fresh, new—and inoffensive—way to tell him no, he said gently, "Please," making it impossible for her to refuse his request without coming off as rude and impatient.

Damn him, anyway. He was good. Too good. The man knew how to work a meeting to his own advantage—and yes, she'd known he would be good. Just not *how* good.

Suppressing a sigh, she rose and circled around to his side of the desk. When she got there, she was careful not to move in too close to him.

"All right," she said. "What is it?" And then she looked at the screen. Her breath caught. "Amazing." The word escaped her of its own volition.

"I was hoping you'd think so."

Captivated in spite of herself, she moved closer. The three-dimensional image could have been plucked right out of her wildest dreams. She was looking at the ideal KinderWay facility. Or nearly so, anyway...

"How did you do that?"

"I hired an architect. I gave him several sources on childhood development and early-learning techniques. I suggested he explore the best facilities around the country—KinderWay included. In my far-from-expert opinion, he did his homework."

She studied the open plan, the large, inviting learning areas: practical life, shapes and forms, mathematics, language... "It's excellent."

"I was hoping you'd say that."

She forgot her intention to keep her distance and leaned toward the image on the big screen, resting a hand on the cool stone of the desktop. "I wonder..."

"Name it."

She could smell his aftershave. Subtle. Pricey. Not that it mattered. "The open area in the center?"

"Larger?"

"Could you?"

"Watch." He highlighted the area. Two clicks and the central activity floor was half again as large.

"There should be a sink here." She pointed to the practical-life section.

He chuckled low in his throat. "I'm not an expert on this program. But I can definitely make a note of that— and look." More clicking and an exterior view appeared. "Separate sheltered entrance," he said, moving the cursor, using it as a pointer. "Note that we'd have it off the hotel area, nowhere near the casino. And…" The image shifted, the view widening to take in… "A protected, completely enclosed play yard."

Enchanted, she leaned even closer. "It looks like a private park."

"That's the idea. And it's even environment-friendly. Most of the greenery is drought-resistant." He clicked the mouse some more. "The pool—"

"The facility would have its own pool?" She couldn't keep the eagerness from her voice. She'd so wanted a pool at KinderWay. But the cost had been prohibitive when she began. And at her current location she didn't have the space to add one.

He made a low sound in his throat. "I thought there could be group swimming lessons, perhaps family get-togethers. You could teach water safety…."

"A pool would be a huge addition to the program." She couldn't keep the excitement out of her voice. "It's a whole other section in terms of life skills."

He chuckled. "Not to mention that in the summer, all Las Vegas kids ought to have a pool."

"Great point." She heard her own laugh rising up, throaty. Warm. She slid him a glance. His silver eyes were waiting....

There was a moment. Time hung suspended, spinning on a shimmering thread. She looked at him and he looked at her....

Somewhere back in her mind, alarm bells jangled. She heard them only faintly.

He said softly, "Your eyes are amber—no, brandy. The color of brandy..."

Straighten up. Step back, her wiser self commanded. She stayed where she was—much, much too close to him. "You're flattering me."

"No. Just stating a fact." He shifted his big body slightly. The movement brought him a fraction closer to her. She saw that there was a distinct ring of icy blue at the outer edge of his irises, making the gray look paler, giving his eyes that otherworldly glow. He said, "Have dinner with me."

She felt...slower, somehow. Lazy. Her heart was beating thickly, as if her blood had turned to honey. *Danny,* she thought. *Remember Danny.* She said, "No. I'm with someone. Someone very special."

"It's only dinner."

"I'm sorry. I can't."

"Brandy-colored eyes. And auburn hair…" He touched her cheek. She didn't stop him. He brushed a finger along the line of her jaw. It was a shocking and inappropriate intimacy, and she felt it through every singing nerve in her body.

She made herself speak. "Take your hand away, please."

He did. Then he said, "Dinner," again, as if she hadn't just told him no. "Strictly business."

"For some reason, I don't believe you." *Straighten up, you fool,* she thought. *Step away from him.* Slowly her body obeyed. One step, two…

He swiveled his chair around until he faced her and then he leaned back—so cool. So casual. "Business," he said again. "We'll enjoy a fine meal and we'll discuss the new KinderWay facility you'll be opening right here at Impresario."

"But that would be a complete waste of your time and mine." He arched a brow, but before he could speak, she informed him—again, "I'm not opening a new KinderWay facility here at Impresario." She stuck out her hand. "Fletcher. It's been a pleasure meeting you."

His lean fingers engulfed hers. "The pleasure was all mine." He gave her hand one firm shake and then released it.

His letting go didn't help. She could still feel the tempting press of his skin to hers. "Goodbye, then." She circled back around the massive desk. At her chair, she scooped up her bag and made for the door.

Fletcher watched her go, admiring the rear view of her tall, curvy dancer's body, appreciating the shine and bounce to that silky-looking cinnamon hair. Once the door had closed—quietly but firmly—behind her, he picked up the phone and buzzed his assistant.

"Marla, get me Brian Klimas." Brian Klimas was a P.I., a damn good one, both thorough and discreet. "And call Tiffany's. Something pretty. A necklace. A bracelet. Either. Have it sent to Ms. Cleopatra Bliss. Her home address. It should be in the database."

"I have it," Marla said. "Is there a message?"

He considered. "Yeah. 'Lunch, then?' With a comma and a question mark."

"A signature?"

"No. She'll know I sent it. Put Klimas through as soon as you get him."

He disconnected and waited. It didn't take Marla long to reach the P.I. Her line blinked.

Fletcher punched the speaker button. "Put him on."

There was a click. Marla said, "You're connected."

Fletcher instructed, "Brian, I want more on Cleo Bliss." He waited, giving Klimas a chance to access his records.

"Got her," said the P.I. "Cleopatra Bliss. Twenty-nine. Owner and Director, KinderWay Preschool. Graduate in child development, UNLV. Put herself through college working nights as a showgirl."

"That's the one. I want everything you can find for me. There's a boyfriend. Check him out—who he is, what he does, how long he and Cleo have been together and how serious the relationship is."

"Anything else?"

"How soon can I get a report?"

"I'll put a rush on it and give you a call tomorrow to let you know where we are with it."

"Good." Fletcher ended the call. As he sat back again, his gaze settled on his computer and the KinderWay design it still displayed.

She'd liked the design. A lot. It had, in fact, provided the moment or two in their meeting where he'd been certain she would say yes to his offer.

All right, then. The design.

Once again Fletcher reached for the phone.

Chapter Two

"So what's in the fancy little box?" Danny Pope asked when Cleo ushered him in the door that evening.

The unopened gift waited, nestled in packing popcorn, in a brown box on the narrow table in Cleo's tiny square of a foyer. She'd found it waiting on the front step when she got home from KinderWay. Once she'd peeled back the cardboard flaps and seen the blue Tiffany box, she'd known who sent it.

There'd been no need to read the card. But she had: *Lunch, then?*

Uh-uh. Not dinner. And not lunch. Not anything. No way.

"It's nothing important," Cleo told Danny. "As a matter of fact, I'm sending it right back where it came from."

Danny frowned. "You know what it is?"

"No, I don't. If I had to guess, I'd say jewelry. The shape of the box seems to indicate a bracelet. Maybe. Or it could be a necklace. Who knows?"

"Well, why don't you open it and find out?"

Cleo took his hand, twined her fingers with his and pulled his arm around her. Settling their joined hands at the small of her back, she kissed him, a quick, firm press of her lips to his. "Nope."

"Why not?" He smelled of a recent shower and also very faintly of motor oil. Danny owned a garage and restored classic cars for a living.

"There's no point," she said. "Whatever it is, I don't want it." She brought their hands back around between them, pressed a kiss to his big, rough knuckles and then turned and headed for the kitchen, towing him along behind.

He pulled her back. "Wait a minute. Who's it from?"

She gave in and said the name of the man she didn't even want to think about. "Fletcher Bravo."

Danny whistled. "*The* Fletcher Bravo?"

She made a show of rolling her eyes. "Please don't tell me there's more than one."

He frowned again—and then he got that adorable, goofy grin that had tugged on her heart from the first day she met him, when her SUV had blown a tire on

I-15 and he'd come to her rescue, her knight in greasy overalls. "Aw, Cleo. Come on…"

She relented. "Okay. Yeah. *The* Fletcher Bravo. I met with him this afternoon."

"Wow. Why?"

"Come in the kitchen. Have a beer. I'll tell you all about it." She pulled on his hand again and that time he went with her.

In the breakfast nook, in front of the bow window that looked out on her postage stamp of a patio and the cinder-block wall enclosing it, she pushed him down into a chair. "Bud?"

"Sounds good."

So she got him his beer, serving it up straight from the bottle, the way he liked it. She explained about Fletcher as she went to work on the salad. "Fletcher Bravo wants me to open a KinderWay at Impresario for the children of selected employees—and more specifically for his soon-to-be five-year-old daughter."

Danny took a long pull off his beer. "You never mentioned anything about Fletcher Bravo before…."

She sent him a look as she grabbed a big knife suitable for chopping lettuce. "Okay. I confess. I've been in denial."

"Denial about…?"

She steadied the head of lettuce on the cutting board and hacked at it with her knife. "Three times I've met with Fletcher's underlings. Each time I've told them, politely but firmly, that I'm not interested." She set the knife aside and scooped up the lettuce she'd chopped, sparing another glance at Danny as she dropped the greens in the salad bowl. "Fletcher wouldn't believe me. I guess that's not especially surprising. He didn't get where he is by giving up without a fight. Finally he asked to meet with me personally. So I met with him. Today." She grabbed a smaller knife and went to work on the radishes, cutting the ends off, slicing them into the bowl on top of the lettuce.

"Wait a minute. You turned him down today—and so he sent you jewelry?"

She paused in midslice, glancing his way, shaking her head. "Doesn't make a lot of sense, does it? To tell you the truth, I still don't think he believes that when I said no, I meant it."

"Cleo?"

"What?" She looked toward him again.

He was picking at the label on his bottle of beer. "I gotta say. If one of the Bravos came to me with an offer to expand, I'd jump at it. The Bravos are big-time. The real deal. Maybe you ought to think twice. This could be a good move for you."

"But I told you. I don't want to do it. I don't like the idea of putting a KinderWay in a casino."

"He wants it *in* the casino? Wouldn't that be illegal or something?"

"All right," she amended, "it would be off the hotel, but still, it's not the kind of location I had in mind." His expression said he wasn't buying. She set down her paring knife. "Okay. Say it."

"Well, it's only…this *is* Vegas, you know? Most of the people who live here work for the resorts and casinos. Those folks have kids, too. And their kids need preschools. And I think, because of how you grew up, you sometimes want to pretend that this is a different town than it really is."

What could she say? He was absolutely right. "Okay. You've got a point…."

He said it again. "This town is what it is."

She kidded him, "Go ahead. Make me face reality."

His sweet smile lit up his face again. "You're welcome."

She flicked on the faucet long enough to rinse her hands, then grabbed a towel and turned to lean against the counter. "This whole thing does get to me. I mean, just because a guy is some big shot around town doesn't mean he's always going to have things his way. If I'm not ready to expand, I'm not ready. Period."

"But this would be on the Bravo Group's nickel, right? You'd get a new facility and they would pay for it?"

"Yeah. So?"

"Well, that sounds like a hell of deal to me."

"How many ways can I say I'm not ready yet?"

Danny took another pull off his beer and set it down with care. "Okay. What's going on?"

She put a lot of attention into thoroughly drying her hands. "What do you mean?"

"You seem really…jazzed about this. Really nerved up. And angry, too."

"Well, I am angry. I've told that man no four times now, including today. And what does he do? He sends me *jewelry*."

Danny's honest brown eyes held hers. "He's after you."

"Didn't we already establish that?"

"I'm not talking about KinderWay right now," Danny said. "I mean *you*." Cleo had no idea what to say then, so she kept her mouth shut. Danny added, "Come on. What guy in his right mind *wouldn't* be after you?"

She let out a hard breath. "Oh, Danny…"

"And why else would he be sending you jewelry?"

She couldn't hold his gaze and found herself looking down, studying the rounded toes of her ballet flats. "It doesn't matter. I'll just send it back."

"You want me to talk to this guy?"

"No."

"You sure?"

She lifted her head and straightened her shoulders. "Yeah. I'm sure."

"You want to…go out with him?"

"Of course not."

Danny smiled. Slowly. "Well, then. We got no problem here, do we?"

She could never resist that smile of Danny's. She felt the corners of her own mouth lifting in response. "You know what? You're right. We've got no problem at all." She turned, hung the towel on the rack and went back to cutting up the salad.

Danny finished his beer and helped himself to a second one. A few minutes later they sat down to eat.

After the meal, they cleaned up the kitchen, working smoothly together, two parts of a well-oiled machine. Then Cleo made popcorn and they adjourned to the living room to catch a movie on pay-per-view.

Cleo shucked off her flats and cuddled up close to Danny, enjoying the strength in his muscular arm when he draped it across her shoulders, thinking that this was a great guy and she'd been lucky—so lucky—to find someone like him.

Someone so sweet and kind, someone who understood her and was always gentle with her and who never, ever tried to boss her around. Someone true and steady and down-to-earth.

Someone totally unlike *some* people she could mention…

When the movie ended, as the credits were rolling, Danny pulled her closer, tipped her chin up and pressed his lips to hers. She kissed him back warmly.

But it was after ten by then and she was tired from the long workday—and the added stress of having to face down Fletcher Bravo.

Danny sensed her mood instantly. He always did. "Tired, huh?"

"Yeah. I guess I am…."

She walked him to the door and they shared another kiss. He asked her out for Friday night.

She said, "I'd love to."

"Pick you up at seven?"

"I'll be ready."

She stood in the open doorway, watching as he went down the front walk and got into his perfectly restored '57 Chevy. He waved as he drove off, and she shut the door, locking it, turning back to lean on it with a sigh—and spotting Fletcher's gift again. She'd have to pack it up and call his office to find out where to send it.

But not tonight.

Tonight she was putting Fletcher Bravo, his unwelcome offer and his unwanted gift completely from her mind.

Ten minutes later she crawled into bed. She drifted quickly off to sleep.

Her dreams that night were thoroughly erotic ones. Danny wasn't in them.

The next morning—Wednesday—she woke up furious. At Fletcher Bravo.

Before she headed for KinderWay, she pushed the little blue box deeper into the packing popcorn and sealed up the flaps with heavy tape. She got the address of Impresario out of the phone book and printed it neatly on the box. She made it in care of Fletcher's secretary, whose name, she remembered, was Marla Pierce. On the way to work she took the box by the post office and mailed it. She felt a whole lot better once the damn thing was out of her hands.

At KinderWay, Kelly, her assistant, asked her how the meeting at Impresario had gone.

"The important thing," she told Kelly, "is that it's done. I told Fletcher Bravo in no uncertain terms that we're not interested in his offer."

Kelly laughed and pretended to fan herself. "That Fletcher Bravo. I've seen the pictures of him in the newspaper and *NightLife* magazine. Total hottie. Those sexy, scary gray eyes of his… Yum. He could make me an offer any day. You can bet I wouldn't refuse."

Cleo was still feeling good that his gift was out of her hands and things were finally settled with him. She joked, "I should have let *you* handle him."

"Oh, yeah. You should have. I'd have handled him and then some."

After that, Cleo did her best to put Fletcher Bravo completely out her thoughts. Friday night, she and Danny went out for dinner and a movie. Saturday, they went to a car show. Sunday, she took the day for herself. She restocked the pantry and straightened the house and went to the mall for a little leisurely shopping. If occasionally the memory of compelling pale eyes crept into her mind, she ordered the image right back out again.

Monday, at a little after ten, with daily classes well under way and the children in each of the three Kinder-Way classrooms absorbed in the study of language arts, Cleo escaped to her office to get a little paperwork done.

The phone rang, and since Kelly was helping out with the three-year-olds that morning, Cleo answered it herself.

"You sent my gift back. Cut me right to the core."

Her pulse picked up speed and a truly exasperating warm shiver went skittering through her. "You shouldn't have sent it."

"You didn't even open it." He was faking an injured tone for all he was worth. "You don't like Tiffany's?"

"Of course I like Tiffany's. Everyone likes Tiffany's."

"But you sent it back. Should I try Cartier?"

She felt kind of breathless. Kind of eager and expectant. Dumb. Really, really dumb. She instructed with great firmness, "Do not send anything more."

Fletcher chuckled, a low, far too sexy sound. "No problem. And now we've got that settled, do you recall the prospective KinderWay design I showed you last Tuesday?"

She admitted warily, "Of course."

"I made the changes you wanted."

The *cojones* on this guy were truly phenomenal. "I didn't *want* any changes. I was only…" She wasn't sure how to go on.

He prodded, "You were only what?"

"Look. It was a terrific design. I got a little carried away, that's all. But I never said I wanted any changes. Why would I? As I *did* say several times, I'm not going to open another KinderWay at this time. And Fletcher, you can't just—"

"Never tell me I can't. It only encourages me."

"But you—"

"Cleo, listen."

Patience, she thought. Calm. And serenity. "Okay. What?"

"I made the changes and I had it built."

For a moment she was sure she hadn't heard right. But then she understood—or so she thought. "A scale model. You've had a—"

"No. Not a model."

"Not a model?" she echoed lamely, still not believing that he could mean what he seemed to be saying.

"That's right. I've had the facility built. To your specifications. In the location we spoke of, off Hotel Impresario."

That was impossible. Wasn't it? "But it's only been six days since—"

"I want you to come and take a look at it."

"I still don't believe that you could possibly have—"

"How about one o'clock? We can have lunch."

"I swear, if you interrupt me again, I'm hanging up this phone."

That gave him pause. At least briefly. Then he said, "I apologize. It's a failing of mine. Impatience."

"Curb it."

He was smiling. She just knew it. He said softly, "On the plus side, I'm a man who gets things done."

"Well. Apparently." She still couldn't believe it. He'd *built* a new KinderWay?

"You really need to see it, Cleo."

She shouldn't. And she knew it. But he was right. She *had* to see this. "Strictly business," she warned.

"Agreed. My office. One o'clock."

Chapter Three

They had lunch at Impresario's five-star Club Rouge, with its light-studded, red-silk-draped ceiling and glittering Swarovski crystal chandeliers. There was champagne. Cristal, 1988. An excellent year, or so the wine steward claimed.

Cleo decided she'd allow herself a glass. Fletcher toasted to the future of KinderWay.

Why not? KinderWay *would* have a future, regardless of its connection with Fletcher Bravo and the Bravo Group. She touched her glass to his. "Bright lights, late nights," she said automatically—and then wished she hadn't.

He set down his glass. He didn't say anything, but

she could see in his eyes that he found her toast out of character.

"My mother used to say that," she admitted grudgingly. "And please don't try to tell me you had no idea my mother was a showgirl."

"All right, I won't." He said it so…mildly.

And that really bugged her. They both knew he was far from a *mild* kind of guy. She set down her own flute and accused, "You've had me checked out. You know everything about me—or at least everything that a good detective could dig up. You have a profile on me, a…dossier, or whatever you want to call it."

"And that bothers you?"

"Yeah. It bothers me, though I get that you want to be sure about whoever you do business with. Especially when it comes to something as important as your child's education."

He sat back in the plush white satin chair. "You'll be relieved to know you checked out just fine."

"Not that I *asked* to be checked out. Not that *I* came to *you*."

"You grew up around the gaming industry. I think you know that the procedure's the same no matter who makes the original approach." He picked up his flute and sipped in a thoughtful way. "Cleopatra. It's an interesting name to give a kid." She only looked at him, tight-lipped. One corner of his fine mouth kicked up in a rueful smile. "It's called conversation. And it's not going to kill you to try making a little of it."

Cleo knew she was being snippy and she ought to snap out of it. After all, she'd agreed to have lunch with him. It wasn't as if he'd forced her to be here.

She picked up her champagne again and drank. It really was delicious. "You would have to know my mother. She came here in the late sixties, from New York City by way of L.A. A trained dancer with big dreams who'd never managed to get much of a start in the movie business or on Broadway. Her given name was Leslie. Leslie Botts."

"Ouch."

Cleo couldn't help smiling. "Not exactly a name to conjure with. She had it changed legally."

"To Lolita Bliss."

"That's right. She was famous in her day—in a minor kind of way, I mean. But then, you already know that. She worked at most of the old casinos, the top ones. The Flamingo, the Stardust, the Sands. She was tall and gorgeous and she knew her stuff. She loved the entertainment business. When she had me, she had no doubt that I was born to follow in her sequined shoes. She named me Cleopatra. She said that 'Cleopatra Bliss' was going to look just grand on a marquee. She used to tell me I would conquer the world. I was three when she enrolled me in my first ballet class. Sometimes we didn't have food in the house, but there was always money for tap lessons and gymnastics."

"And you turned your back on all that to open a school."

"That's right."

"Was your mother okay with that?"

"She died when I was nineteen. She never knew I chose a different career than the one she had planned for me."

"Would she have been disappointed?"

"To say the least—but I like to think she'd have gotten over it eventually."

"And your father?"

She turned her crystal flute by the stem. "My mother raised me without a father—and didn't your detective tell you that?"

One dark brow lifted. "More or less."

She chuckled, though not really with humor. "I thought this meeting was supposed to be strictly business."

"It is."

"Then why all the personal questions?"

"I'm interested in you."

Now why did those words send a naughty little thrill zipping through her? "My mother never would tell me who my father was."

"Why not?"

"See? You're getting way, way too personal."

He didn't appear the least apologetic. "The way I look at it, I can't lose by asking. If you give me answers, I've got more information than I had before. If you don't, well, I'm no worse off than I was in the first place."

She took another small sip of bubbly—and told him a little more of what he wanted to know. "My mother knew a lot of men. She preferred the rich and powerful.

High rollers, preferably whales." A whale, in casino terms, was a gambler who could afford to lose millions. She went on, "Wheeler-dealers. She liked a player who was playing with a nice fat bankroll. A lot of her men were already taken, if you know what I mean."

"Married."

"That's right."

"You make her sound like a heartless home wrecker."

"Do I?" Cleo frowned. "Well, as I said, there *were* a lot of men. But heartless? Uh-uh. She was…passionate and glamorous and she loved living large. She was always falling in love and then getting her heart broken. She just couldn't seem to stop herself from hooking up with the wrong kind of guy."

"But you're not like that." Was he being sarcastic?

She couldn't tell—and, she reminded herself, his attitude didn't matter to her in the least. "That's right. I'm not like my mother. When I look down, I see two feet firmly planted on the ground."

"Did you ever try to find your father?"

"Not exactly."

"Now what does that mean?"

She smoothed the napkin she'd already laid in her lap. "I don't think I'm going to answer that one. Which is fine, right? Leaves you no worse off than before you asked the question."

He leaned a little closer, those pale eyes seeming to see right down to the center of her. "You found him," he said at last with an absolute certainty that sent another shiver running down her spine—this one not nearly so warm as the shivers before it. "Your father is Matthew Flint." Matthew Flint was a Las Vegas legend. He'd been building supercasinos in the eighties, back when the biggest place around was the MGM Grand. And yes, he was Cleo's father.

She demanded, "Why are you asking me when you already know?"

"I'd like to hear it from you, that's all."

She probably shouldn't have told him. It didn't concern him in the least. But still she found herself explaining, "My father found *me*. In my mother's hospital room the day before she died. He'd heard she had pancreatic cancer. By then, she'd been through both chemo and radiation. The tumor hadn't shrunk much and cancer was all through her body. She was wasted down to nothing and she'd lost all her beautiful blond hair. She hated that the most. She was always so proud of her hair...."

He prompted softly, "And your father?"

"The word got out she wouldn't make it. My father knew it was his last chance to see her. So he paid her a final visit. I was there at her bedside when he showed up."

"And you've kept in touch with him since then."

"As you know, he already has a family. A wife. Two sons. I try to keep it low-key, you know? But now and then we get together."

"I understood that he backed you when you started out."

"Yes. He's the main reason I was able to open my own preschool at the age of twenty-five." She found herself thinking that she ought to turn the tables on him and ask a few questions about *his* absentee father, Blake Bravo. Like almost everyone else in Las Vegas, Cleo had read the articles about the fabulous Bravo brothers and their swift rise to prominence. Always there was mention of their father, the notorious sociopath who had faked his own death at the age of twenty-six and then gone on to romance an endless number of gullible women—with the classic result: Blake had left illegitimate children all over the good old U.S. of A.

Fletcher said much too softly, "We have a lot in common."

And before she could argue, let alone get him talking about his father, a waiter appeared and set their green-bean-and-crayfish salads in front of them.

Fletcher gave the waiter an approving nod. "This looks wonderful, Armand."

"Enjoy, Mr. Bravo." The waiter beamed them a big, bright smile.

"Armand is a single father." Fletcher sent Cleo a meaningful glance. "He has a three-year-old son, a little boy named Alain who is very much in need of a quality preschool."

Armand nodded, a quick dip of his dark head. "My Alain is a bright child. He needs a challenge. Day care isn't giving it to him."

"But then," Fletcher chimed in right on cue, "a good

preschool can be so expensive—not to mention that there's often a waiting list. Plus, there's the difficulty of getting the kids to and from where they need to be. If we could provide a preschool here, on-site, at a significantly reduced rate to our employees, it could make a lot of difference to a number of hardworking, concerned parents like Armand."

"Ah," said Cleo as if she hadn't heard all this in their previous meeting a week before. The waiter nodded again and left them. She looked at the man across from her. So brilliant. So dynamic. "So sneaky," she said.

He picked up his fork. "It's true. When I want something, I pull out all the stops to make sure I get it." His look said that KinderWay wasn't *all* he wanted.

She felt that sexy, shimmery sensation beneath her skin—and willfully ignored it. "How many more employees with needy preschool-age children will I be meeting this afternoon?"

"A few," he replied with an easy shrug. He tipped his head toward her plate. "Eat your salad. It's excellent. More champagne?"

"One glass is my limit—especially around a world-class operator like you."

After lunch they went through the glittering casino at the heart of Impresario, a casino housed in a giant red windmill several stories high. From outside, the massive vanes of the windmill turned, crisscrossed with thousands of bright golden lights. Inside, visitors looked up at a wide dome painted the color of night and studded with a thick blanket of gleaming artificial stars.

As they crossed the busy casino floor, Fletcher stopped now and then to introduce her to certain employees: a dealer, a security staffer, a cocktail waitress. Not the least surprisingly, they all had young children. And they all worked long hours. They really *needed* a service like the one she could provide....

They left the casino and emerged onto a fully enclosed, cobbled imitation-Parisian street. As they strolled along between the bright-colored, shuttered facades of fake buildings, she told him, "You are shameless."

He answered without the slightest hesitation. "You bet I am."

Cleo had suspected she would be impressed with the facility he'd managed to have built in such an impossibly short period of time. But *impressed,* as it turned out, was too mild a word.

The play yard surrounded the classrooms, so any children who went to school there would look out on a garden—a garden landscaped in succulents and other plants that would thrive in an arid climate. There were just enough patches of grass to make it inviting. Bougainvillea climbed the high stucco fence, softening it, and there was a large playground, complete with jungle gym, slides and a giant-size sandbox. He'd even included several drought-resistant trees: magnolias, sweet gums, red maples.

The Olympic-size pool—dug, but not poured yet— had its own fence, for safety. Fletcher showed her where the separate boys' and girls' cabanas, each with showers and restrooms and grooming areas, would go.

He led her inside the main building, from one classroom to the next. Each was just as they'd discussed that day in his office, with large central areas, generous supply closets and accessible learning stations. The many chalkboards and expanses of cork walls for pinning up displays weren't installed yet, but they would be up tomorrow, he said. Each class had its own storage and coatroom, with nice big cubbies for every student. Finally he took her down a hallway to the administration area and she saw the room that would be her office—*if* she agreed to his plans.

Which she wasn't going to do.

Was she?

Somehow, as the afternoon sailed by, it got harder and harder to remember all the reasons she'd taken a firm stance against opening a KinderWay at Fletcher Bravo's resort.

"After you." He pushed open the door to the director's office for her.

She went in. Across from the door, a big window looked out on the play yard. She crossed to it. As she stared through the glass, it seemed she could almost hear childish laughter, see the happy kids swarming the slides, hanging all over the giant jungle gym and the big wooden play structure, spinning on the carousel, swinging on the swings, crawling through the tube tunnels that snaked around the sandbox....

"You approve?" Fletcher asked. She turned to face him. He stood several feet away, beside the wide, well-made desk. He put his lean hand on the desktop. "Italian walnut. Nice clean lines. I thought you might like it."

She told him honestly, "It's beautiful. Ideal. And I wouldn't have believed it was possible. All this. So quickly..."

"Anything's possible. With a good plan, the right people—"

She cut in. "—and enough money."

He shrugged. "That goes without saying."

"Well. I'm...amazed."

He dropped his gaze and for a split second he almost seemed shy. "Good."

And she was in big trouble here. In a moment she'd be saying yes to his offer. How could this have happened? "Fletcher, I really think—"

He cut her off for the first time that afternoon. "I'd like you to meet my daughter before you make your decision."

But I've already made my decision, she thought. She didn't say it, though. Somehow, right then, she just couldn't. Right then, to say it would have been too cruel somehow.

Clearly this meant a great deal to him. Much more

than she'd imagined the first time she'd met with him. During that other meeting—was it only last week?— she'd been certain that his commitment to KinderWay would never be more than temporary at best.

But this office, that play yard, the open, welcoming classrooms he'd just led her through…

He might have had it all built with remarkable speed, but none of it seemed temporary. Far from it.

She said, "The years go by fast. Your little girl will grow right up and out of here. What would happen to KinderWay then?"

"We'd have a contract. You'd be in charge here. I have a strong suspicion you'd make certain that the Bravo Group held up its end of our commitment to the program."

She almost smiled. "No doubt about that."

Those pale eyes gleamed. "So it wouldn't be my commitment that mattered, would it?"

"When you put it that way, no. It wouldn't."

He ran his palm over the desktop again. "Do you want children of your own, Cleo?"

The question seemed far too personal. Still, she answered him truthfully. "Yes. I'd like about a dozen kids. But that's probably going to be impractical, so I'll settle for two or three."

Something happened in his eyes. She wasn't quite sure what. He said, "When you have kids, things change. You…see things differently. Before Ashlyn came to live with me, I hardly gave a thought to the child-care needs of the people who work for me. But now I find I don't work at optimum level if I'm worried about Ashlyn. So I thought…" He let the sentence trail off as if he knew she could finish it for him.

She did. "If *you* worry about Ashlyn, your employees are probably concerned about their kids, too."

"That's right. So I did my homework. I dug up the results of several studies correlating dependable child-development programs with the parents' job performance. I brought those results before the board. Since the board approves anything that will boost our bottom line, my plan got approval. Even better, the chairman of the board—"

"Your cousin, right? Jonas Bravo?"

"Yes. Jonas liked my proposal so much that he decided to set up a foundation to help fund it."

"A not-for-profit?" Cleo folded her arms across her chest. "There are a lot of rules controlling a non-profit business."

"Relax. Jonas set up the foundation to fund the facility itself—meaning the physical plant, everything I've just shown you, the classrooms and the play yard and the landscaping. The KinderWay program, including the day-to-day operation of the school, which belongs to *you,* will be run as for-profit, just the way you run your other facility."

She realized they were discussing this as if it were a done deal, as if she fully intended to hire a staff and run his preschool for him.

But it wouldn't be his *preschool,* she found herself thinking. It would be hers. It would be KinderWay. Yes, taking on a project of this size would be a challenge. She'd have to be careful not to spread herself too thin.

Then again, to grow any business, the boss needed to learn how to delegate. And a lot of kids would benefit from the exceptional program she could provide here....

She let her arms drop to her sides. "We're getting way ahead of ourselves."

He looked at her, a long look, one that affected her in dangerous ways. At last he said, "Come on. Meet my daughter." He took her arm. She felt the touch of his hand all through her, a shudder of awareness that centered down to a warmth deep within.

She didn't pull away.

Fletcher lived in a penthouse suite on the top floor of Hotel Impresario's central tower. The elevator let them off in a hallway paneled in a rich dark wood with a striking wood-inlaid stone floor. Overhead, an oval skylight let in the winter sun.

"This way," Fletcher said.

A set of big double doors led into a private foyer. The foyer widened at the opposite end, opening onto a living room with floor-to-ceiling windows providing sweeping city views.

Fletcher took her hand again and wrapped it over his arm. She was far too conscious of the heat of his strong body so close, of the clean, expensive scent of him, of the hardness of his forearm beneath the fine fabric of his beautifully made suit jacket.

He led her away from the living room, through another opening to their right. They walked down a hallway, past a marble-walled kitchen on one side and an elegant dining room on the other, into a family room with walls upholstered in some warm reddish-brown fabric and comfortable-looking soft sofas and chairs.

A little girl sat cross-legged on the kilim rug in the middle of the room. She wore blue capris with pink piping at the hems and a lime-green T-shirt, also trimmed in pink. On her small feet were pink socks with green appliqués and pink Keds. A book lay open across her knees.

She looked up as they entered and regarded them with shining, oh-so-serious brown eyes. "Hi, Daddy." She closed her book. "I was reading Livvy *The Funny Little Bunny.*"

A plump, friendly-looking blond girl rose from an easy chair not far from the child. "Hello, Mr. Bravo. We've just been reading a bit before Ashlyn goes down for her nap."

Fletcher said, "Cleo, this is Olivia, Ashlyn's nanny." Cleo and the nanny smiled and nodded at each other.

Ashlyn jumped to her feet and held out her little hand. "And I'm Ashlyn. I'm almost five."

Cleo took the small fingers in hers. She looked into

those big brown eyes and she wanted to pull the child close, to press a kiss to the sleek crown of her head.

She couldn't help herself. She was captivated by Fletcher's bright, beautiful, oh-so-serious child. There was something about Ashlyn that reminded Cleo way too much of herself as a child, something in her solemn manner, in those wide, too-wise eyes.

Ashlyn said, still in that grave way of hers, "You're pretty. And very *tall*."

"Why, thank you, Ashlyn."

"You're almost as tall as my Daddy, I bet."

"Just about."

"You can let go of my hand now."

"All right." She released the small, soft fingers.

Ashlyn put both hands behind her back but held her ground, dark head tipped back, those serious eyes scanning Cleo's down-turned face. "It's nine days." She brought her hands front again and held up all her fingers, small face puckered up. Then she bent her right thumb to her palm and turned both hands, backside-first, to Cleo. "Nine."

"Very good."

"It's arithmetic."

"Yes. What's nine days?"

"Until my birthday. I'm having a party. Not *on* my birthday but the Saturday after. There will be clowns and rides and a magic show. A lot of kids are coming." She seemed to reach a decision. "You can come, too."

"Why, I…"

"There will be cake."

"Well, that is tempting."

"And ice cream." Fletcher spoke from behind her.

Cleo looked back at him and knew by his carefully composed expression that he was hiding a smile. "Devious," she muttered.

He said, "Whatever it takes."

She turned back to the child. And Ashlyn asked, so simply and sweetly, "Will you come to my party?"

Cleo said the first word that popped into her head. It just happened to be, "Yes."

Fletcher insisted on escorting Cleo to the parking garage and out to her car.

Neither spoke as they got off the elevator they'd taken from his apartment and crossed to the ones that went to the parking garages. They got on an empty car and went down to C level. When the doors slid open, she turned to him.

"It really isn't necessary for you to—"

"But I want to." He signaled her to exit ahead of him and then fell in beside her once the elevator door had shut behind them. Their footsteps echoing on concrete, they walked the five rows to her green SUV.

Cleo had her key ready. She pushed the remote lock button. The SUV beeped twice, the sound very loud in the cavernous space.

She made the obligatory polite noises. "Thank you. It was an excellent lunch."

He moved in closer—too close, really. She saw again

the blue that rimmed those pale gray irises. She smelled that tempting aftershave. She might have moved away a step, put a little space between them. But the SUV was at her back.

He said, as if continuing a conversation that had never been interrupted, "So many children here and at High Sierra who can gain so much from what you have to give them…"

Again she tried to remember all the reasons it wouldn't work to put a KinderWay in his resort. Those reasons seemed meaningless now. "I can't believe I'm thinking of saying yes to this."

"Believe it. Say yes."

"There are…permits and procedures we'd have to—"

"We'll cross every T in sight, dot every last damn I."

"I'll have to hire an entire second staff, start from the bottom up. That will take—"

"It's manageable. All of it. And it won't take long. Believe me."

She felt a silly smile tremble across her mouth. "You're interrupting me again."

"Sorry. Did I tell you I'm impatient?"

"You did. Yes."

"You won't regret this, Cleo. That's a promise."

It all seemed so simple by then. From all wrong to exactly right in the space of a few hours. Was that crazy? Maybe.

Then again, no. Not crazy at all. It was a fabulous opportunity and *she'd* be crazy to pass it up.

"Come on," said Fletcher. "Say yes." He held out his hand.

She took it. "Yes," she said, those forbidden, hot little flares of awareness racing through her at his touch.

"Excellent." He gave her hand a firm shake and then released it. "I'll call you tomorrow. We'll set up a meeting ASAP with the lawyers, get all the paperwork handled. Then you can get started looking for the people you'll need." He reached around behind her, grabbed the door latch and pulled it open for her.

Feeling suddenly dazed, she swung up into the seat. She stared at him wide-eyed. "Did I just say yes?"

He grinned. "You did. No going back now." He pushed the door shut and stepped back.

For a moment, still bemused at the choice she had just made, she only sat there and stared at him through the side window. He lifted an eyebrow, clearly wondering if for some reason she'd changed her mind about leaving.

Feeling foolish, she shook herself and stabbed her key into the ignition. The engine turned over and caught. She backed out of the space, so rattled by what she had just agreed to that she came within an inch of hitting a car in the row behind her.

She slammed on the brakes and looked over at Fletcher, who still stood where she'd left him.

He mouthed the word, "Careful."

She put it in drive and got the heck out of there. Every nerve in her body was humming. Very strange. Definitely scary.

And no, she didn't let herself look in her rearview mirror to see if he was still standing there watching as she drove away.

Chapter Four

That night in bed, before she turned out the light, Cleo called Danny and told him that she would open a KinderWay at Impresario after all.

"Good for you," Danny said.

She relaxed into her pillows, realizing she'd been vaguely worried he wouldn't like the idea, that he might be a little jealous, might remember that blue box on the entry hall table last Tuesday night and suspect that Fletcher Bravo would be putting the moves on her. But no. Not Danny. He didn't have a jealous bone in his body.

"Oh, Danny. You think so? You really think it's the right way to go?"

"You bet. I think it's a smart move. And I'm glad you

decided not to let what happened when you were a kid keep you from accepting a great offer right now."

She caught a curl of her hair and wrapped it around her index finger as she teased into the phone, "Who says I was doing anything as neurotic as that?"

"Hey. I didn't say it was neurotic."

"Close enough."

"Aw, come on. It's natural for a person to stay away from the things that scare them, the things that have messed them over in the past. It only gets to be a problem if you let what scares you keep you from doing what's going to be good for you now."

Sometimes Danny's insights did amaze her. "You know, I think you missed your calling. You should have been a shrink."

"Uh-uh. You need a college education for that. I'll pass. I had enough trouble makin' it through high school."

"If you say so. It's the mental health profession's loss."

"Yeah, right."

"And Danny?"

"Huh?"

"I wasn't scared. Did I say I was scared?"

"You didn't have to say it. There was no reason for you to turn down such a great offer—except that you'd have to be around the business that you always say wrecked your mom's life."

There's another reason, a knowing voice in the back of her mind whispered.

That other reason was Fletcher Bravo himself. A man

way too much like the men Lolita Bliss could never resist. A man with power. With juice, as they say. A man who liked a challenge, liked the chase, liked going after a woman he thought he couldn't have…

And just a second here. How the heck did she know if Fletcher Bravo was that kind of man? Yes, he had power and influence. But that didn't necessarily make him a dog. He wasn't married. He was an eligible bachelor. Of course he would date. He could go out with a different woman every night if he wanted to and no one had a right to judge him for it.

And why was she obsessing over Fletcher anyway? Really, she had to stop thinking about him.

If Fletcher Bravo gave her a thrill, so what? She was going nowhere with it. She was sticking with Danny, who was exactly the man she'd been looking for all her life.

"Cleo? You still with me."

"Yes. I am."

He laughed his goofy laugh. "I like the way you say that."

They talked some more. He told her about a beautiful old Mustang he was restoring. She described the fabulous facility Fletcher had had built in the blink of an eye.

Danny was so sweet and supportive. "Sounds good, Cleo. Really good…"

Before they said good-night, they set a date for dinner Wednesday.

The next morning at ten, Fletcher called her at Kinder-Way. "Can you make it at two to go over the contract?"

"I'll need to have my lawyer look it over first."

"You think you need a lawyer, do you?"

"I wouldn't sign a contract without consulting one."

"Good answer."

"How about this…I'll come in and pick up the papers. I'll take them to my lawyer. If I don't have any questions, I'll sign them and bring them back."

"Fair enough. Come at one. We'll have lunch."

"You don't miss a beat, do you?"

He made a low sound. It might have been a chuckle. "Rarely."

She hesitated. And then she felt silly. It was only lunch, which she'd be eating in any case. She agreed to meet him at High Sierra's Placer Room, where the food was supposed to be almost as good as at Club Rouge.

Again there was champagne.

"To celebrate your decision to bring KinderWay to Impresario," Fletcher said as the wine steward poured.

Like the day before, Cleo only had one glass. What did she need with alcohol anyway? She was flying high naturally, feeling giddy and excited at the prospect of the big job she'd taken on. It *was* the right time to expand, she realized now. And she couldn't wait to get things moving, get that gorgeous new facility staffed and ready for the kids who needed it.

Once they'd ordered and the waiter left them alone, Fletcher wanted to know more about her childhood and about the shows she'd been in while she'd worked her way through college.

She shook her head. "Uh-uh. Your turn."

He tried to put her off. "I know all about *my* life. I want to hear about yours."

But she wasn't letting him push her around. She repeated, "Your turn."

He gave in and told her that he'd been born in Dallas. "My mother was working the graveyard shift at the Pancake Palace. Blake Bravo came in for a cheese omelet with sausage and a short stack on the side. For her, it was love at first sight."

"And for Blake?"

"No way to say. He was gone in the morning and she never saw him again—not until about thirty years later, when she opened her morning newspaper and saw his picture under the headline Notorious Bravo Dies for the Second Time."

"Your mom raised you on her own?"

"For the first ten years she did. Then she met my stepdad. They married and we moved to Ocean City. My stepdad serviced vending machines, had his own little business—still has it and does all right at it, too. They have two daughters, my half sisters, Cathy and Anna-Marie. Cathy's at NYU and Anna-Marie is a senior in high school." His expression had softened.

"You're crazy about your sisters." That pleased her.

"Yes, I am." He said it with real enthusiasm. "Cathy's studying microbiology. And Anna-Marie says she wants to be a writer—at least right now. She's at that age where it's always something new."

"I wish I had sisters. Or brothers. I'm not picky. Family counts, you know?" Her hand rested on the snowy tablecloth.

He laid his over it. "I know."

She felt the warmth of his skin against hers and she wanted to…

No. Uh-uh. Not going there.

Carefully she pulled her hand away.

As they were leaving the restaurant, they stopped off at a corner table and Fletcher introduced her to his half-brother Aaron and to Aaron's wife Celia, who was also Aaron's personal assistant.

Celia, who had a cute heart-shaped face and red hair, was pregnant. Very pregnant. She looked as if she'd swallowed a watermelon, as if she would have that baby right then and there, over lunch. She confided, "Our oldest, Davey, is just three. He'll be attending your school." She put her hand on her huge stomach. "And so will this one, when the time comes." Her hazel eyes twinkled. "I'm so glad you decided to bring KinderWay here."

"I'm pretty excited about it myself," Cleo said.

At her side Fletcher laughed—a low, knowing laugh that played along her nerve endings. "To hear her talk now, you'd never guess how hard I had to work to convince her she needed to do this."

Aaron held out a hand. "Welcome to the Bravo Group family."

Cleo took it and they shook. She met Aaron's blue eyes and wondered what he might be thinking. Like the Bravo standing beside her, it was hard to figure out what could be going through his mind.

Fletcher put a hand—so lightly—at the small of her back. "Okay, we'll let you two enjoy your lunch in peace." Cleo went where he guided her, stunningly aware of the press of his palm against the base of her spine.

They took the elevator to the office tower. As they stepped into the car, Cleo eased away from him. She turned and backed against the brass railing that ran along the mirrored elevator walls.

They looked at each other, neither of them speaking. She found herself achingly aware of how small the space was, how with only a step or two she would be in his arms.

Crazy. Ridiculous. She was not, under any circumstances, going to end up in Fletcher Bravo's arms.

She shifted her gaze and she was looking at her own reflection in the mirrored wall behind him. Did she look as guilty as she felt?

Before she could decide if she did or not, the elevator whooshed to a stop and the doors parted.

Marla had a manila envelope all ready for her. Cleo took it with a smile. "Thanks."

From behind her Fletcher said, "I'll see you to your car."

No way, she thought, as she turned to him. She made a joke of her refusal. "You don't want to do that. You saw the way I pull out of parking spaces. I might actually run over you this time."

"I'll take my chances."

Danny had said it that night last week: *He's after you.*

And he was. He *still* was: his hand on hers at the table; his palm settling so possessively at the small of her back as they left the restaurant...

Subtle, knowing touches. What a man does to draw a woman in. Nothing obvious. Nothing blatant. Making it so very easy to pretend it isn't happening...

But it was happening. And she had to stop denying, stop pretending it wasn't.

Guilt tightened her stomach as she remembered how she'd assured Danny that she wasn't interested.

Liar, she silently accused herself. She *was* interested. She just didn't want to be—no. Wrong, damn it.

She wasn't *going* to be. She was stopping this slow and oh-so-clever seduction, stopping it right here and now.

She drew herself up. "No," she said firmly. "I enjoyed the lunch. Thank you."

He held her gaze for a second too long. She felt the heat zipping back and forth, arcing between them. And then he said silkily, "No need for thanks. I'm pleased that we're going to be working together."

Cleo saw her lawyer the next morning. The lawyer said everything looked good, so she took the signed papers back to Impresario that day. She made a point of *not* calling first, which meant she ended up handing the

envelope over to Marla, who promised to see that
Fletcher got it right away.

That duty discharged, Cleo returned to her office at
KinderWay and started making lists, getting her prior-
ities in order for all the work that lay ahead.

Fletcher called at three. "You should have told me
you were stopping by."

"No reason for that." She spoke much too briskly. "I
only dropped off the contract."

He was silent. But not for long. "You'll need keys
to the facility. Did you want to conduct your interviews there?"

Her face felt hot. She laid her hand against her cheek.
Blushing. Definitely. This was so absurd.

"Cleo?"

She realized she hadn't answered him. What *was*
the question?

Oh, yeah. About the interviews…

"Well, I thought I could hold the interviews here. I've
got everything set up and operating. And my current
staff will be available to help me."

"Makes sense."

"I will need those keys, though. I've got office equipment to purchase. And supplies. And furniture—tables
and chairs, all that. I'll need to be able to get in and out
of the facility."

He said, "I'll have the keys waiting for you. Check
the concierge desk at the hotel. Just show them ID."

"Hotel Impresario, you mean?"

"That's right."

He'd have them waiting....

He wasn't offering lunch, wasn't inventing excuses for them to get together. Apparently he'd gotten her message loud and clear: keep away.

Good. He was the wrong kind of guy for her and she was glad he'd realized the two of them weren't going anywhere.

He said, his tone all business, "Since you signed the contract without asking for any changes, I'm taking it that you agree to the opening day we proposed. You'll be ready to open the doors on February fourteenth?"

The fourteenth was two and a half weeks away. It was also Valentine's Day, as luck would have it. For some reason, that struck Cleo as terribly ironic.

"I'll do my best," she told him. "It's cutting it pretty tight."

"You signed the contract." He said it gently.

Annoyance prickled through her. Did he have to rub it in? But then she reminded herself that he was only stating a fact. "I know. I'm a little worried about the background checks, though. I run background checks on everyone I hire, even the ones who are already licensed. But the checks can take time...."

"Are the checks really necessary? If they're licensed already, I would think that would do it."

She wasn't backing down on this one. "There are a lot of reasons KinderWay is the best. We go the extra mile. All of our teachers and care providers are not only highly skilled and well trained, they've also been thoroughly vetted. We can say that we've done everything humanly possible to be certain no predator or abuser gets near any of the children in our care."

He must have been convinced; he didn't argue further. "Let me speed that up for you, then."

"That would help. How?"

"Call Klimas Investigators. They're the best. Talk to Brian Klimas himself. Give him the names of all your prospective hires and tell him what kind of check you want done on them. Tell him that you need a rush on it. And tell him to bill the Bravo Group."

She wondered if he'd hired this Brian person to check *her* out. But she didn't ask. "All right. I'll call him."

"Anything you need, just let me know."

"I'll do that. Thanks."

"We'll want a progress report midway—say Friday, the fourth?"

"Certainly."

"Just to see that we're on track."

"Yes. Of course. No problem."

"You won't have to report to me. Talk to Darlene Archer in Human Resources. I'll see she's up to speed on what we're doing. She'll call you at the beginning of next week and set up a time the two of you can meet."

"That will be fine."

"Also, I'll see that Darlene has a check ready for you tomorrow, to cover any early expenses you incur. Set up accounts with any stores or suppliers you'll be using regularly. They can bill the Bravo Group. Again, talk to Darlene. She'll tell you what you need to know and answer any questions that come up."

"I will. Don't worry…."

He actually laughed then. It was a warm, wry sound and it made her wish she could…

But no. Nothing was going to happen between them. She was happy with Danny, with her life as it was.

He said, "I'm not worried, Cleopatra. Not worried in the least."

"Well, okay, then. Good."

"One more thing and I'll let you go."

She clutched the phone a little tighter, realized she was doing it and consciously relaxed her grip. "Sure."

"Ashlyn's birthday party is on Saturday, the fifth. From noon to five at Circus Circus, the Adventuredome." He added drily, "No one can ever say I don't support the competition."

Ashlyn's birthday. She'd almost forgotten. Or, to be honest, she'd *let* herself forget. Because contact with Ashlyn meant contact with Fletcher, and she was seriously conflicted about that.

And yet, she *had* promised the solemn-eyed little girl….

And come on. Really. She was essentially in business with Fletcher now. She would be running into him now and then. There was no avoiding it.

And even if she never had a reason to talk shop with him again, even if she always went through Darlene in

HR from here on out, he'd be showing up at KinderWay every day to drop off his daughter, for crying out loud.

Fletcher said, "I hope we'll see you there."

"Of course I'll be at Ashlyn's party," she replied. "Please thank her for inviting me and tell her I'll see her at the Adventuredome."

"I'll do that. Goodbye, then."

"Goodbye, Fletcher."

The line went dead. Cleo hung up and told herself she didn't feel the least bit sad or at all let down.

When Fletcher finished the unsatisfying call to Cleo, he had another call waiting. He took it without checking to see who it was.

"Fletcher? There you are, at last."

"Andrea." Andrea Raye was a featured dancer in the erotic revue, *Cancan du Bal,* which had been playing at Impresario to sell-out audiences for the past six months.

Andrea laughed, a charming sound, one that was only a little bit forced. "Where have you been? I haven't seen you in *weeks.*"

He supposed he should have a talk with her. "How about lunch tomorrow?"

"I would love lunch. Or you could just come by after the show tonight." She pitched her voice lower and suggested seductively, "We'll have breakfast—eventually."

He spoke gently. "Thanks, but that's not going to work."

"Ah," she said after a lengthy pause. "I get it." There was a deep sigh. "So this is it, huh?"

"Andrea…" He never knew what to say at this point.

She laughed again, the sound more brittle than before. "Oh, please. We're both adults, now aren't we?"

He knew that whatever he said next was bound to sound lame. And it did. "Yes. We are."

"I'm thinking that lunch will be a little too…after the fact, if you know what I mean."

"I understand."

"Will you send me something pretty, to remember you by?"

"Absolutely."

"Diamonds. I really like diamonds…."

Andrea's out-front request didn't surprise him in the least. When his half brother Aaron had been single, before Celia had turned him into a die-hard family man, there had been a lot of women. The story went that Aaron would always give them diamonds when he said goodbye. Word had probably gotten around. Vegas, in a lot of ways, was a very small town.

Hell. He could almost hear the women whispering, *I got diamonds from Aaron. What did Fletcher give you?*

"Fletcher? Is…that okay?"

"Diamonds it is."

"Oh, thank you—and Fletcher?"

"Yeah?"

"I have to tell you. I'm gonna miss you…."

He wished her well and said goodbye.

Then he buzzed Marla and told her to see that Andrea got her diamonds. After that, he called Darlene in HR and briefed her on her new responsibilities with the KinderWay project.

He didn't like having to do that—didn't like giving up the various opportunities for contact with Cleo that holding on to the KinderWay connection would provide.

But Fletcher Bravo knew when to fold 'em. He knew that a better hand would come his way eventually. Cleo had been as much attracted to him as he was to her. There was no denying heat like that.

Not forever.

All he had to do right now was wait. Lady Luck would find him in her own good time.

She always did.

Chapter Five

Danny took Cleo to Black Angus that night. Right after the waitress served their prime rib dinners, he asked if something was wrong.

For a moment she couldn't quite meet his eyes. She stared down at her huge baked potato and the mound of sour cream exploding from it. "Good thing I'm not dancing anymore. After a dinner like this one, I'd get kicked off the show at the next weigh-in."

Danny refused to let her change the subject. He asked softly, "You gonna answer my question, Cleo?"

She made herself look at him. "Oh, really. Nothing's wrong. Nothing at all. Why?"

"You seem...I don't know. Kind of sad."

"But I'm not sad. Not in the least." It came out sounding way too vehement. She smiled to show him it was no big deal.

He shrugged. "Maybe just distracted, then?"

"Well, okay. A little…"

"Over the deal with Impresario, right?"

She answered lamely, "It's a big step."

"Cleo?"

"What?"

"Relax. You're going to do just fine."

She beamed him an even bigger smile. "Somehow you always manage to say just the right thing."

He came in for coffee when they got back to her house. As she was filling the drip basket with fresh-ground decaf, he came up behind her and wrapped his strong arms around her.

She jumped in surprise.

"Hey," he whispered, smoothing her hair out of the way and pressing his lips to the side of her neck. "It's only me…."

"No kidding." She turned in the circle of his arms and rested her hands on his chest.

He whispered, "You're so beautiful. And I'm crazy for you…." His mouth touched hers.

Cleo kissed him back. But her heart wasn't really in it.

Danny knew it. He pulled away and gave her a rueful smile. "Not in the mood, huh?" He was too much of a gentleman to mention that she hadn't *been* in the mood since a little over a week ago. Since the day she'd met—

She cut that thought off before it went any further. This had nothing to do with any other man. A whole lot had happened in the past week. She was taking on a huge new project. It was only natural that she would be a little bit distracted....

"Danny, I'm sorry. I—"

He laid a light finger against her lips. "Shh. It's okay." He stepped back. "Go on, make that coffee."

She felt as though she ought to say something, to explain herself somehow. But she didn't want to make a big deal about this. Because it *wasn't* a big deal. She was busy and preoccupied and, well, Danny had said it himself: just not in the mood.

Turning back to the coffeemaker, she finished loading the basket.

In the days that followed, Cleo hit the floor running every morning and collapsed into bed exhausted every night.

She bought equipment and supplies, reworked the program guidelines for each of the classes, tweaking and improving so she could start out with the best study blueprint possible at the new location—*and* keep things fresh and exciting at the original school, as well. She called a big meeting with her current staff, explained her plans for expansion and asked for volunteers to move to the new location. The idea was to take at least a few experienced people over to Impresario so that the new facility wouldn't be starting with all new hires. It worked. Two teachers—she had six teachers in various capacities at the original location—and three aides said they'd be happy to make the move.

Cleo knew that to expand effectively, she was going to need a really good associate director, someone who could step in and hold down the fort at one location whenever Cleo was needed at the other. Fortunately she found just the right woman for the job on the first day of interviews. A former elementary school assistant principal, Megan Helsberg had the right education and training, the right experience and excellent references. She was also available to start immediately.

Brian Klimas's security check on Megan came back clean, so Cleo had Megan work with her to hire the rest of the new staff. Megan caught on quickly, but her job duties were varied and complex; there was a lot for her to learn. Cleo trained her as they worked—all while continuing her director's duties at the first KinderWay and preparing the Impresario facility for its grand opening on Valentine's Day.

Cleo and Danny hardly saw each other. There was simply no time. Once she finished a day's work on the new facility, she had to play catch-up at the old one. She was at her desk every night until after ten, determined to keep up her standards at the existing KinderWay and also to honor her contract with the Bravo Group to deliver a top-quality service and to open the doors to the new facility on time.

Cleo and Megan met with Darlene Archer on Friday,

the fourth, in the HR offices at Impresario. Darlene was impressed with the progress they'd made. Cleo promised they'd be ready to open on the fourteenth— and realized as she made that promise that they had a very good chance of making it.

Darlene gave them the access code to the student list. It contained all the basic information on the students who would be showing up for preschool on Valentine's Day, including emergency phone numbers and a health profile for each child. With that code, she already had all the information usually gleaned from the endless forms that parents filled out at enrollment. The new KinderWay would be operating at capacity from the first day it opened its doors.

Saturday, Cleo went to Ashlyn's birthday party at the Adventuredome.

Fletcher, looking heartbreaker-handsome in a light cashmere sweater and dark slacks, greeted her with a cool smile. "I'm glad you could come."

"I'm so pleased Ashlyn invited me."

They traded a few more generic pleasantries. As she made the obligatory small talk, she felt…desperate, somehow, just at the sight of him, at the sound of his deep, tempting voice.

Yes, desperate. And sad.

My God. I've missed *him.*

As quickly as the thought took form, she banished it. He turned to greet another guest, and Cleo moved away, into the group of kids and parents that had formed nearby while they waited for everyone to arrive.

For the rest of the afternoon she kept her distance from the father of the birthday girl. It wasn't all that difficult; he made no effort to get close to her. She watched Ashlyn and her friends take on the junior rides—the Frog Jump and the Miner Mike roller coaster and the miniature airplane ride. She enjoyed the magic show and the clowns. There were also "family" rides, where the kids needed an adult to ride with them.

For one of those, a Ferris wheel called Drifters where the cars looked like hot-air balloons, Ashlyn ran up and slipped a small hand into hers. "Cleo. Ride on the big balloons with me, please?"

Cleo looked down into those serious eyes and all at once her chest was too tight to contain her heart. There was just something about Fletcher's little girl, something so sweet and honest and special....

Ashlyn was frowning. "Cleo? Are you sad?"

Was she sad? It was the question Danny had asked her more than once—and also the way she had felt when she'd faced Fletcher again today for the first time in over a week.

Cleo smiled. "Right now I'm just…happy for you." She squeezed the little hand tucked so trustingly into her own. "Congratulations on being five years old."

Ashlyn's frown faded. "Thank you." A few feet away Fletcher boosted a little boy onto his shoulders—a little boy with blue eyes and the cutest kid-size cleft in his chin. "That's my cousin, Davey," Ashlyn explained. "He's three. Sometimes he makes me crazy, but mostly he's all right. Daddy has to take care of him because Aunt Celia couldn't come to my party after all. She had to have a baby yesterday."

So Celia had delivered her baby at last. "Wow. That's exciting. Boy or girl?"

"A girl. She's my new cousin and her name is Jillian Jane. She got her name from Aunt Celia's two best friends in the whole wide world, my aunt Jillian and my aunt Jane. But my great-aunt Caitlin said the baby looked like a J.J. That made everybody laugh, though I don't really understand why it was funny. After that, they all called her little J.J. It's her Nick name, Daddy told me. That's kind of funny, huh? You get another name and it's called your Nick name even though you don't even know anybody named Nick?" Ashlyn frowned again. "I don't have one."

"A nickname, you mean?"

"That's right. I don't. Do you?"

"Yep. My nickname is Cleo."

Ashlyn's big eyes got even wider. "Then what's your *real* name?"

"Cleopatra."

Ashlyn tested the word. "Clee-o-pat-ra. It's very long."

"Cleopatra was once the queen of a country called Egypt."

Ashlyn considered. "A queen? Really?"

"Yes."

"I like Cleo better."

"Good. Because that's what everyone calls me."

"Did you know that I'm going to go to your school?"

"Yes, I did."

"My daddy told me. Livvy's leaving next week and I will go to your school when she's gone. I'll miss Livvy lots, but I think I'm getting old enough that I should be going to school."

"I'm very pleased that you'll be one of our students—and I think we just missed our balloon ride."

"Oh, that's all right." Ashlyn tugged on Cleo's hand. "Come on. We can get in line and ride the next time...."

They ended up riding with Fletcher and Davey. The kids laughed and cried out in delight as they rose toward the pink Adventuredome sky—and Cleo tried not to let her gaze collide with Fletcher's.

Later, before the cake and ice cream, Ashlyn opened her presents. Cleo had given her a stack of books—some by Dr. Seuss and some by Shel Silverstein and one of Cleo's personal favorites called *Goodnight, Moon.* Ashlyn tore off the bright birthday paper, let out a glad cry and then jumped down from her chair. She rushed over to Cleo and held out her arms. Cleo bent down and Ashlyn grabbed her around the neck in a tight hug.

"Cleo, how did you know I love books?"

"Easy. The first time I saw you, you were reading *The Funny Little Bunny* to Olivia."

"That's right. You come over to my house, okay? I'll read to *you.*"

Cleo was far too aware of Fletcher sitting across the

big round table. She made the mistake of glancing his way. He was looking right at her.

She met those haunting eyes and she felt it—that familiar heat burning beneath her skin. Her heart stuttered, then started racing....

She tore her gaze from his and focused on Ashlyn again. "You'll be going to my school soon, remember?"

"Acourse I remember."

Cleo smoothed the silky brown hair. "You can read to me there, at school."

"Okay. I will." Ashlyn grabbed her in another hug and planted a big wet kiss on her cheek. Then she returned to her chair and the pile of birthday presents still waiting to be opened.

Ashlyn really was something, Cleo found herself thinking, so thoughtful and mature for her age. Fletcher's daughter exclaimed over each gift as she opened it and seemed sincere in her excitement every time. She didn't come across as spoiled in the least—and that was surprising. In Cleo's experience, children of doting wealthy parents tended to get big attitudes early on.

After the presents came the cake. They all sang the birthday song. Then Ashlyn made her wish and blew out her five candles in one breath. Olivia and another young woman worked together to serve up the cake, piling generous scoops of vanilla ice cream on top.

It was five o'clock in no time. Cleo got another hug from Ashlyn and said a quick thank-you and goodbye to Fletcher and she was out of there.

That night Danny asked her again if something was wrong. Again she told him there was nothing. She saw in his eyes that even he, so patient and always understanding, was growing tired of the way she avoided his touch.

After he left, she lay awake much too late, hating herself for not treating him right, actually beginning to admit that the best and most honest thing to do would be to break things off with him.

And no, she had no intention of getting anything started with...anyone else. But Danny was such a fine man. He deserved a woman who couldn't keep her hands off him. Cleo wasn't that woman. At least, not anymore.

She had a while to think it over. Danny left town Sunday for two big car shows, one in Phoenix and a second in Southern California. He wouldn't return until the fifteenth or sixteenth. By then, the new KinderWay should be open and operating. Things wouldn't be so hectic. She would sit down with him and they would talk it out, come to a real understanding—one way or the other.

The week sped by, as stressful, busy and exciting as the one before it. Cleo and Megan worked straight through the weekend.

Their efforts paid off. On Monday, the fourteenth of February, KinderWay at Impresario opened its doors.

Cleo had opted to spend that first morning going from classroom to classroom, checking out the various first-day welcoming activities, seeing that everything ran smoothly. She happened to be in the three-year-olds' room when Celia Bravo dropped Davey off. She had her new baby with her.

Cleo went straight for that baby. "I hear you're calling her J.J."

Celia sighed. "I'm afraid so."

"May I...?"

Celia beamed her a wide smile. "Absolutely."

So Cleo held out her hungry arms and Celia laid the warm bundle in them. Cleo gazed down at the bald pink head, the rosebud of a mouth and the tiny turned-up nose. "Beautiful..."

"I think so," Celia agreed. "But then, I *am* her mother." Celia turned to kiss Davey goodbye, but her son was already occupied, playing blocks with a couple of the other kids. She cast Cleo a wry glance. "As you can see, he can't get along without me."

"Looks like a well-adjusted boy to me."

"And I'm glad he is—but a big hug and a kiss goodbye would be nice."

Davey turned and waved. "'Bye, Mommy. Come back and see me soon."

Cleo, who couldn't bear to let go of that warm pink bundle just yet, suggested, "Come on, I'll walk you out."

They ran into Fletcher in the central breezeway that connected the classrooms. He'd just dropped Ashlyn off with the five-year-olds. He greeted Cleo and Celia and remarked that things seemed to be off to a great start.

"So far, so good." Cleo glanced up from J.J.'s sweet

little face and into the eyes that haunted her dreams. Quickly she looked down at the baby again.

Celia said, "Cleo got her hands on my baby and now she won't let go."

Cleo laughed and smoothed the pink blanket, then stroked one plump and perfect little hand. "Oh, don't I wish…" And then she made the mistake of glancing up a second time. Her laughter faded as her gaze locked with Fletcher's.

Trouble, she thought. *I'm in big, big trouble here.*

She made herself turn to Celia. "I suppose I'm going to have to give her back to you…."

Celia took the baby and they started for the nearest of the three gates that led out to the parking lot behind Hotel Impresario. Along the way they passed other parents with their kids. They waved and shared greetings as they went by.

When they got to the gate, Fletcher put his hand on Cleo's arm. She felt that touch far too acutely, as she'd felt every one of his touches since that first day they'd met. "I need a few minutes."

Carefully she pulled her arm free. "Sure."

"This is where J.J. and I came in." Celia left them, taking the sidewalk around the KinderWay fence, heading toward the hotel. More parents with children approached the gate.

Fletcher took her hand, capturing her fingers, wrapping them around his arm. "How about your office?"

"All right." And she let him lead her, as if she

didn't know the way, back through the gate and along the breezeway.

She knew she should probably pull away again. But she didn't. She kept thinking it shouldn't matter as much as it did—the touch of his hand on hers, the feel of his warm, hard arm beneath the fine fabric of his suit jacket, the heat of his lean body so close to her side.

They entered the main office. The new secretary, RaeAnne, smiled as they passed her desk. "Cleo. Mr. Bravo…"

"We'll just be a few minutes, RaeAnne," Cleo said. "No calls or interruptions. Not unless there's bleeding involved."

"Got it."

Cleo let go of Fletcher's arm—and felt her heart contract at losing hold of him.

No doubt about it. Trouble. Capital T.

"This way." She opened the door to her office and ushered him inside, gesturing at a guest chair. He sat and she went to her chair behind the beautiful desk he'd had built just for her. "Now," she said, sounding brisk and businesslike and feeling anything but. "What's up?"

He studied her for a moment before he spoke. She felt his gaze as if it were a physical touch. At last he said, "You've done an amazing job with this project. I didn't really believe you'd succeed in doing what you've done here—not in two and a half weeks, anyway."

She couldn't resist reminding him, "I believe you chose the time frame."

He gave her one of those regal nods of his. "I did. I like setting impossible goals. They make people try harder. And you did." Another regal nod, then he said, "Well done."

"Thank you." So. He'd only taken her aside to give her a pat on the back for the work she'd done.

That was good. She was pleased. He wasn't putting any moves on her and she wanted it that way.

Too bad she felt so let down.

He asked, "Aren't you glad now that I wouldn't leave you alone until you agreed to go for it?"

To her, the question had more than one level of meaning. She reminded herself not to go to those other levels. "Yes, I am. It's worked out beautifully."

He slid a hand into the inside pocket of his suit coat and produced a red leather jeweler's box embossed with gold.

Another gift.

Well. So much for a purely professional pat on the back. Damn him. She had told him not to—

"Don't," he said, as if she had spoken her objections aloud—which she hadn't. Yet.

"Fletcher, I asked you not to—"

He raised his free hand for silence as he set the red box on her desk. "Open it."

"No."

Her refusal didn't faze him in the least. "All right. I'll open it for you." He took the box again, raised the lid and set it down facing her so she could see what waited inside.

A watch. White gold or maybe platinum, with a black

alligator band. A small, oh-so-tasteful row of diamonds running down either side of the square face and the single word *Cartier* beneath the upper numerals. A go-anywhere watch. Gorgeous and simple and absolutely perfect.

And very, very expensive.

He explained, "It's engraved on the back with the date and 'KinderWay at Impresario'—and don't look at me like that. Yes, it's a gift. A strictly professional one. To commemorate a job much more than well done."

Strictly professional. Did she believe him?

Yes. No. She didn't know.

She did know that the watch was beautiful and she had done a hell of a job in the past weeks and…yes, she wanted it.

What did that make her? A professional justifiably proud of her latest accomplishment? Or a woman finally saying yes to a man's slow, relentless seduction?

Or both?

The really scary thing was that it didn't matter what it made her. Whether this gift was strictly professional or not, she was keeping it.

Her doubts fell away. She knew at that moment that she would have to break up with Danny. And that someday soon Fletcher would ask her out to dinner again. And when he did, her answer would be yes.

No qualifications. And no restrictions. Simply, completely, yes.

She picked up the box and removed the watch, turning it over, reading the inscription, which was just what he'd said it would be. "Thank you," she said for the second time. "It's an important day and now I have something to remember it by." She laid it over her wrist and caught the tiny diamond-studded buckle to clasp it.

"Let me...."

She started to refuse—and then stopped herself. What good would refusing him such a small thing do her? In the end, she would say yes to everything. She understood that now. And her intuition told her that the man across from her had always known, from that first day when she met with him in his office. He had always known...and he had been right.

She extended her wrist to him.

He stood. It took him only a moment to hook the delicate pin into the buckle. He held on a few seconds longer than necessary. "It looks good."

She met his eyes without wavering as those now-familiar sensations of heat and longing danced beneath her skin. "Yes. Thank you again."

With obvious reluctance, he released her. "And I have to go." He waited for her to rise and come around the desk. When she did, he fell in behind her. It was only a few steps to the door.

She felt him acutely at her back. She wanted him. She'd tried to deny it, but the wanting did not go away. So she was yielding to it, finally, her capitulation at last complete—so much so that she almost stopped in midstep and turned to him and...

No.

Not here. And not now.

She had come to the point where she realized what was bound to happen, where she even accepted it. But not today, not in her office. And most important, not until she'd talked to Danny and told him goodbye.

Still, she simply couldn't resist turning back to Fletcher as she opened the door to the outer room. "I *am* glad," she conceded. "That you kept after me. That it's worked out so well."

He took a long time to answer—sizzling, delicious seconds during which heat shimmered in their shared glance. "I'm pleased, too. Very much so," he said at last, and they both knew he referred to more than KinderWay.

She leaned back against the open door and allowed it to happen—for one more sweet, seductive moment before he left her, to get lost in his beautiful, dangerous eyes.

Then, with a slow sigh, she turned back toward the outer room. And blinked in guilty horror at what she saw.

Danny.

He was sitting on the sofa against the wall opposite Rae-Anne's desk with a heart-shaped box of candy in his lap.

"You have a visitor," said RaeAnne.

Danny took the box of candy in his beefy hand and stood. "Hey. Got home early." His soft, dark eyes took it all in: Cleo standing stunned in the doorway and the tall, commanding, beautifully dressed man behind her. "Thought I'd drop by and see how things are goin'."

Chapter Six

Danny understood in an instant what Cleo had refused to accept for nearly a month. He kept it calm and low-key, shaking Fletcher's hand when Cleo introduced them, even smiling that sweet, open smile of his. The two men exchanged a few quick words of greeting and then Fletcher took his leave.

Danny followed her into her office, but he didn't sit down. The minute she shut the door, he set the box of candy on the credenza and said, "I think we really gotta talk."

"Of course. Danny, I—"

He put up a hand. "Not here, okay?" She swallowed and nodded. "I'll be over tonight. Eight o'clock."

What could she say? Nothing. Except, "I'll be there, Danny."

"All right, then." He left without another word.

She took the box of candy out to RaeAnne and told her to share it with the staff. Cleo didn't eat a single piece herself. She couldn't.

Her doorbell rang at eight exactly. Danny looked so somber when she let him in.

She offered, "Are you hungry? I could…" She didn't know how to finish. His expression broke her heart. It was infinitely gentle and much too wise.

"I didn't come here to eat and I think you know that."

So she led him to the living room. He took the easy chair and she perched on the edge of the couch.

He got right down to it. "Since that night I came for dinner and saw that little blue box—the one you wouldn't open—I been getting the picture, getting the feeling there was someone else. I kind of figured it might be the guy who sent you that box, might be Fletcher Bravo—and it is, isn't it? I knew it today, when you two came out of your office…." He seemed to run out of words. In the silence he just looked at her, waiting for her to answer him.

She felt about two inches tall. "Danny, I swear to you, I never went behind your back. Not with anyone. I would never do something like that."

"I know you wouldn't." He gave her the kindest, most tender little smile and she wanted to cry then, just bawl her eyes out. But she held the tears back. After all, she wasn't the injured party here. "You're not that kind of woman," he said. "And I know that you loved me— or at least, you thought that you did."

"Danny, no. I *did* love…" She cut herself off. She couldn't go on, not with the way he was looking at her, both knowing and disbelieving at once.

He shook his head. "I always knew that you *wanted* to love me, that I'm the kind of guy you think will be good for you, the kind of guy you're gonna feel safe with. The kind of guy who's nothing like the high rollers and big shots who messed your mom over so many times. And you know what? That was enough for me, to be the one you could count on, to be the guy you could trust, until…well, until now. Until I saw you today with a guy you're crazy for."

She longed to argue, to stand up and say, *No, Danny. I'm not crazy for Fletcher. Not in the least.*

Too bad she couldn't get her mouth around such an enormous lie.

Danny said, "You been pulling away from me for weeks. You been *tired* every time I touch you. You know that you have."

"I know. I'm so sorry…." She felt like a total creep, too awful to look him straight in the eye. She dropped her gaze.

He got up from his chair and came to stand over her. "Hey."

She tipped her head back and made herself meet those kind eyes and realized that it wouldn't be right, wouldn't be fair, to keep saying how sorry she was. Sorry just didn't cut it. She swallowed and sat up a little bit straighter and said with real regret, "I'll miss you, Danny."

"And I'll miss you. But Cleo, the way you looked at that guy…"

She swallowed. Hard. "Yeah. I know."

He pointed at her wrist. "He give you that watch?"

"Yes. Today."

"And you took it."

"Yes, Danny. I did."

"I think you're in love with him. Are you?"

"Oh, Danny…"

"You know what? Don't tell me. I don't need to know."

And that was it. There was nothing more to say except, "I'd better get your things…."

He shoved his hands in his pockets, lifted a shoulder in a half shrug. "Yeah. Okay."

So she got up and went to collect his spare razor and toothbrush from the bathroom, his blue windbreaker from the hall closet. "I think this is all of it." She handed everything over.

"Thanks."

She opened the door for him and closed it quietly as soon as he had stepped through.

And then she returned to the living room and sat down on the sofa and couldn't believe what she had just done. She'd said goodbye to Danny, her best friend, the man she had been so certain would one day be her husband and the father of her children. Danny, the exact right man for her, good and honest and true.

She sat there alone on her sofa and wondered which was worse: that she'd lost the sweetest guy she'd ever known, that she was actually *relieved* that Danny ended it—or that Danny was right. Somehow she'd gone and let herself fall for Fletcher Bravo, a man who was everything she'd sworn *never* to fall for.

It occurred to her that maybe she was more like her mother than she'd ever let herself admit. Now there was a seriously scary idea. It wasn't as if all the hard lessons had faded from her mind. Uh-uh, they were with her, still fresh and vivid and full of pain.

She could close her eyes and see Lolita now—at three in the morning, standing in the doorway of the bedroom they'd always had to share since there was never money to "waste" on a two-bedroom place. Every spare penny had to go to headshots and building their portfolios, to hair and makeup and killer clothes and the endless series of dance lessons.

Oh, yeah. Cleo could still see her mother now: Lolita Bliss, standing in the bedroom doorway, the light from the hallway behind her falling on her platinum-blond hair, making a halo effect around her shadowed face….

"Baby, you up?" Lolita whispered—a stage whisper loud enough to wake Cleo if by chance she had been sleeping.

Cleo dragged herself to a sitting position, squinting against the bright hallway light. "Yeah, Mom. What?"

And her mother came dancing in, smelling of Joy

perfume and Max Factor and something else—something
musky and thick: sex, though Cleo hadn't realized it then.

Lolita dropped with a happy giggle to the edge of the
bed. "Oh, darling. It's happened. It's happened at last.
I've met him. My own real-life Prince Charming. He's
rich and he's so handsome and he can't take his eyes off
me—not to mention his hands." Another throaty giggle
escaped her, followed by a long, dreamy sigh. "Oh, honey,
he loves me already." Lolita held out her arms, wiggling
her fingers. "Come on. Come here." And Cleo moved
closer, into the warmth of her mother's supple, sculpted
body and those mingled smells of perfume and makeup
and sex. Lolita hugged her so tight and whispered against
her hair. "Cleopatra Bliss, our lives are about to change
big-time. You'd better believe it." Her mother's long, lean
dancer's arm squeezed her harder. "Say you do."

"I do, mom," Cleo lied.

"Say it again. Please…"

"Mom, I do."

Her mother's lips brushed her hair. "Oh, sweetheart,
he'll make everything good for us. Just wait. You'll see…."

But their lives didn't change. And the men came and
went, each of them breaking her mother's heart when
he left her.

And Cleo grew up dreaming of an ordinary life—a life
where her kids ate three square meals a day, where they
went to bed at a decent hour and woke up at daybreak
and Cleo cooked them all a nutritious breakfast. In Cleo's
dreams, she lived in a real house and everybody had her

own bedroom and Cleo's husband was a good man, a regular, down-to-earth guy, both steady and true.

A guy exactly like Danny, as a matter of fact—Danny, who had just said goodbye and walked out the door.

So what about Cleo's lifelong dreams now? She'd never have the life she longed for with someone like Fletcher. And please, who was she kidding? It was highly unlikely she'd have *any* life with Fletcher. He *wanted* her, period. And she wanted him.

This thing between them had nothing to do with the two of them building a life together. So if she couldn't forget about him, she'd better learn to accept that what they'd have together wouldn't last all that long.

Cleo supposed it was funny in a grim sort of way. Here she sat, contemplating the brief white-hot affair she and Fletcher would share. She was heading right into the kind of nowhere relationship her mother had never been able to resist. Lolita, though, had always believed that each player she fell for was finally the *right* one, that she'd found *him* at last.

Not Cleo. She was cursed with a crystal-clear view of hard reality. Fletcher Bravo was no knight in shining armor. With him, it would be hot and heavy and over-whelming…and brief.

The more Cleo thought about that—about how she was following in her mother's footsteps without the benefit of her mother's stubborn and somehow valiant il-lusions—the more she resisted her longing for Fletcher.

As the week went by, she tried to keep from running into him. In the morning and in the afternoon, when the kids were picked up and dropped off, she stayed away from the five-year-olds' classroom and off the breezeway where she could easily cross paths with him coming or going.

She avoided him—and she longed for him. She daydreamed about kissing him. And at night her dreams went way beyond mere kisses.

On Thursday, she happened to be in with the three-year-olds again when Celia brought Davey in. J.J. wasn't with them.

"Where's that beautiful little girl of yours?"

Celia grinned. "Up at the apartment."

Since Cleo had access to Davey's student file, she knew already that Celia and her family lived in one of the big penthouses at the top of High Sierra Hotel. She couldn't resist asking, "You like it...living on-site?"

Celia leaned a little closer and whispered, "I wouldn't have it any other way. And J.J.'s with her aunties, Jilly and Jane. They refused to part with her even long enough for me to come down here and drop Davey off at school."

Cleo remembered what Ashlyn had revealed at her birthday party. "Jilly and Jane. J.J.'s named after them, right?"

Celia nodded. "They're my best friends. We grew up together, up north in the dinky little town of New Venice. Our husbands are New Venice natives, as well. They all

had bad reputations as those wild Bravo boys. We—
Jilly, Jane and I—were very, very good girls. It's the
classic story, I guess. A bad boy and a good girl. Sparks
flying. Love. And marriage. Though I must admit, when
I fell in love with Aaron, I never imagined we'd end up
husband and wife. He so was *not* the marrying kind, if
you know what I'm saying…."

Cleo did know. She nodded and made an agreeable
noise in her throat, feeling wistful. Celia and her friends
were not only happily married to Bravo men, they'd also
lived the kind of childhood that Cleo had always longed
for. "I know New Venice. It's not far from Lake Tahoe."

"That's it—and hey, why don't you come on up to
the apartment around noon? You'll like Jane and Jilly.
And Jane is cooking lunch for us. She's a genius in the
kitchen. I guarantee the food will be fabulous."

"Oh, I couldn't…."

"Yeah, you could. Come on. Say yes."

What could it hurt? And Cleo was curious about the
other two Bravo wives. Plus, she'd liked Celia from the
first time she'd met her at the Placer Room that day she
and Fletcher had stopped by their table. "You know
what? I'll be there."

"Great. We'll set a fourth place."

Jane Elliott Bravo, who had long, corkscrew-curly
black hair and owned a bookstore in New Venice, was
five months' pregnant and thrilled about it. "It's our
first," Jane announced, a proud hand on her swelling

stomach. "Cade wants a little girl. I'll take either. As long as she's healthy, that's all I ask."

Jillian Diamond Bravo, a fashion plate in black and white with ropes of pearls, black tights and Mary Janes, was an up-and-coming lifestyle columnist in Sacramento. She was holding the baby when Cleo joined them. Jilly gazed adoringly down at the little darling. "I love being an auntie. But a mother? Well, not quite yet." She beamed them all a broad smile and then grinned at Cleo. "I can see it in your eyes. You want to hold her."

"You are so right."

So Cleo took the baby, who waved her plump arms and yawned enormously, then promptly dropped off to sleep. Celia took her and put her in her crib and they all sat down to eat.

Lunch was every bit as good as Celia had promised: an incredible salad of baby greens and glazed pecans, followed by a main course of crawfish étouffée over rice. After the meal, they retired to Celia's sun-bright living room where the view rivaled the one in Fletcher's apartment across Las Vegas Boulevard at Hotel Impresario. Jane and their hostess sipped herbal iced tea while Jilly and Cleo indulged in second glasses of an excellent white wine.

Cleo knew she probably should have said no to that refill. The wine was making her just a little bit tipsy. But for the first time in days she found herself actually having a good time.

"I'm glad I came," she confided. She sipped some more. Delicious. "Though the hard truth is that now I'm having a second glass of this wonderful Chenin Blanc, the rest of my workday will be pretty much shot."

Celia looked slightly smug. "That was exactly my plan."

Cleo laughed. "To get me drunk?"

"No, to get you to take a few hours off. I'll bet by now you need a break." She turned to the others and briefly explained the job Cleo had tackled and successfully completed in the last few weeks.

"Pretty darned impressive," said Jilly. "Here's to you, Cleo."

Jane added, "We are so pleased that you came to lunch."

"Oh, me, too," said Cleo. "You have no idea how much I needed this."

They all rose, clinked glasses and drank.

Just as Cleo was about to sink back into her comfortable chair, Jilly caught her wrist. "Cleo. This watch... Cartier. Oh, I knew it." She laughed. "I really, really *need* one of these."

"It is beautiful," Jane agreed.

Cleo looked around at the friendly faces of the three women she was so glad to be getting to know—and her throat clutched up tight on her.

She felt tears rising. How ridiculous. She gulped and blinked, trying to force them back down. But they wouldn't go.

"Oh, honey," said Jilly, her dark brows drawing

together in real concern. "What did I say? I'm so sorry...."

Cleo grabbed Jilly's hand. Tight. "No. Please. It's not you, honestly. It's only..." Her throat locked up tight then, and the silly tears spilled over.

Jane reached for her. Never had another woman's open arms looked so...necessary. With another huge sob Cleo fell into that warm and welcoming embrace. She bawled on Jane's shoulder, soaking her soft red sweater, feeling the bulge of Jane's pregnant belly nudging her own flat stomach. Jane rubbed her back and the other two women made cooing, understanding noises.

"It's okay...."

"Don't worry."

"Just cry if you need to."

"Just let it all out...."

Jane guided her back to her chair and eased her down into it, and Celia handed her a tissue. Cleo swabbed her eyes and blew her nose and told them, "Oh, I can't believe this. I never cry like this." She sobbed some more, took another tissue, blew her nose again.

"What is it?" asked Jane so gently. "What's got you upset?"

"Yes," Jilly urged, "you can tell us."

Celia tried a joke. "What happens in my apartment *stays* in my apartment."

They were all so dear and they really did seem to care and, well, Cleo needed to tell someone, she truly did. She sniffed and swiped at her eyes. "It's Fletcher."

There. She'd said his name right out loud. She said it again. "It's Fletcher. That's the sad, awful truth."

"Fletcher," echoed Celia in a knowing tone. "I should have guessed."

Cleo wiped her eyes some more. "It's just…I'm so crazy about him and he wants to go out with me and, well, I know he's all wrong for me." She blew her nose a third time and told them everything—from that first meeting in Fletcher's corner office to how she'd pushed him away for weeks and then finally taken his gift of the watch and how Danny, who was the perfect man as far as she was concerned, had broken it off with her because he knew she'd fallen for Fletcher.

When she'd finished her sad story and accepted another tissue from Celia, Jane dropped to the arm of her chair and bent close, that cloud of dark hair swinging forward around her arresting face. "Listen. Don't feel too bad. I know, it's awful when you fall for a Bravo man." Jilly and Celia were nodding—in total agreement, apparently. "All of them," Jane went on, "the sons of Blake Bravo, they always seem to have…issues, you know? They all grew up without a father and their childhoods had big challenges and…that's just how they are. Kind of tough to get close to. At first, anyway…"

"But Cleo," said Celia, "you might be surprised if you gave it a chance. You might find out that Fletcher is exactly the right guy for you."

Cleo blinked. "You're not serious."

Celia looked slightly crestfallen. "Well, yeah. I was. Kind of…"

"Celia, he's a major player. You know it." She pointed her tissue at Jane and Jilly. "They know it. See? They're not arguing. My mother loved nothing *but* major players and I know one when I see one. Fletcher's a gorgeous guy with lots of power and a boatload of money, and I know he's got a different girlfriend for every day of the week."

Was she hoping they'd disagree with her—just a little, at least? No such luck.

Celia did go so far as to wave a dismissing hand. "Well, Aaron was that way, too. The drop-dead beautiful women came and went so fast I could hardly keep track of them. And as his personal assistant, it was my *job* to keep track of them. I was like you then, sure he was never going to settle down with one woman—and if he did, not with *me*. I'm very happy to tell you that I was totally wrong. It could be that you—"

"Wait a minute," Jilly cut in. "Look, Cleo. We are so not going to tell you what you should do."

"Well, *I* am," Celia insisted.

Jilly shot her sister-in-law a warning look and continued, "We're not going to lie to you. We all find Fletcher a hard guy to know."

Celia was scowling. "But I think—"

Jilly cut her off again. "Ceil, come on. Fletcher's a smooth operator, totally charming when he wants to be. And loyal where it counts. I believe he'd lay down his life for anyone he called family—or for anyone he considered his responsibility, for that matter. But what goes on inside that brilliant mind of his? It's not like any of us knows." She gave Cleo a game smile. "All we can say is, we did marry his brothers. And each one of us was certain our love was never gonna work. And look at us now."

Cleo slumped in her chair. "The problem is, I'm just…paralyzed. Can't stop thinking about him, can't seem to make myself face him. I've actually been kind of hiding out from him, never going anywhere I might run into him during the time he would be dropping off or picking up Ashlyn…."

Celia pointed her index finger skyward and declared, "Action. Sometimes it just comes down to the fact that you have to do *something*, you know what I mean? Make a choice and go for it."

"But with honesty," said Jane. "Look him straight in the eye and lay the truth right on him."

Jilly chimed in again. "Action is good." Jane gave her a sharp look and she shrugged. "Yeah. All right. Honesty matters. I know that, Jane. But Cleo, you still have to figure out what's going to work for *you*. If you decide to go to him, can you live with it if it ends up just the way you're afraid it will? On the other hand, can you stand *not* to give what you feel for him a chance?"

"Oh, Jilly…" Cleo sniffed and dabbed her eyes some more. "Those are the right questions. I just don't know the answers."

"You will," said Jane. "Trust me on this. Eventually you'll make a choice."

"Make it soon," advised Celia. "It took me forever to tell Aaron how I felt about him."

"And?" Cleo asked, daring to hope she'd get reassurance.

Celia looked sheepish.

Jilly spoke for her. "It went badly. *Really* badly."

"Gee. Great to know."

Celia sat up straighter. "But soon enough things did improve. Greatly. Looking back, I only wish I hadn't dithered around so much."

A half an hour later Cleo left Celia's penthouse. She paused at the door to exchange business cards with Jilly and Jane. And, of course, to hug each of the Bravo women in turn.

"Call us," said Jilly. "Any of us—*all* of us—anytime you need to talk."

Cleo promised that she would.

The wine and the uncharacteristic crying jag had left her feeling draggy and tired. She would go home, relax, watch a movie on Lifetime. After weeks of driving herself day and night, an afternoon of doing nothing was just what she needed.

She got in the private elevator that serviced Celia's suite, forcing a weak smile for the attendant and then standing back against the far wall of the car, trying not to look at herself in the gold-veined mirrors that surrounded her.

The attendant cleared his throat. "Parking levels?"

Her car was parked across the street, behind Hotel Impresario, not far from KinderWay. "No. Fifth floor please. I've got to go back over to Impresario."

"Fifth floor it is." The car hummed, picked up speed—and slowed to a stop in no time at all. "Here you are." The door rolled open.

Cleo left the elevator, walking at a brisk pace. She had a ways to go, around to the front of the resort to the open area where the escalators carried people up from High Sierra's casino and then across the glass skyway that connected the two resorts at fifth-floor level.

At Impresario she took the escalator down, hurried through the noisy, busy casino and along the fake French streets. At last she reached the hotel. She passed the long check-in desk and started down the hallway that led to the back parking lot and, at last, her SUV.

By then, she was looking down, focused on moving fast. She wanted out of there and into the privacy of her car. She had no idea who was coming toward her until he was standing right in front of her.

She spotted the gleaming pair of fine Italian shoes first. The shoes stopped a few feet from her, directly in her path. She started to dodge around, looking up at the same time—right into those mesmerizing pale gray eyes.

She stopped stock-still and drew in a sharp breath. "Oh, no," she muttered. "Not *you*. Not right now."

Chapter Seven

Great, Fletcher thought. He hadn't seen her since Monday and now he finally ran into her, all she could say was, *Oh, no. Not you*....

But then he looked closer. Her eyes were red and slightly puffy. She must have been crying not too long before. What the hell was that about?

Concern replaced frustration. "Cleo, what's wrong?"

"Nothing. And you know, I really have to go." She tried again to dodge around him.

He slid to the side and blocked her. "Wait." He wasn't letting her go without knowing what had happened, without finding out if there was something he could do to help.

"Fletcher, please…" She was looking at the red-and-gold carpet again, as if she couldn't bear to meet his eyes.

What the hell was going on here? He knew that the people hurrying past on either side were staring, wondering the same thing—not that he gave a damn. Let 'em stare.

He took her by the shoulders. "Cleo, come on. Tell me what's happened." She tried to turn her face away—but he caught her chin and tipped it up to him. "Your eyes are red and swollen. You've been crying. Did somebody—"

She didn't let him finish. "No. Nobody." She tried to jerk away. He held on. And then she pinched up that soft mouth he couldn't wait to kiss. "All right," she said. "Fine. If you must know, it's *you*."

That kind of startled him. "Me? But I haven't even seen you since Monday. How could I—"

"Stop." She hissed the word at him, red-rimmed eyes flashing.

"But I—"

She got a hand between them, waved it in his face. The rows of diamonds on the watch he'd given her the other day glittered in the light from the crystal chandelier overhead. "Just stop," she commanded in a hot whisper. "Just listen."

Fine with him. "Okay. What?"

"Let go of me."

He didn't want to let go. He *never* wanted to let go. He had a feeling she was only going to turn and stride away from him on those incredible long legs of hers. And he was fed up with waiting for his chance with her, tired to the bone of biding his time, of keeping it cool with her, when all he wanted was to take her down in flames.

"Let me go, Fletcher."

Reluctantly he took his hands away and dropped them at his sides.

She didn't run. Instead she drew herself up, straightening those fine shoulders, pointing that pretty chin high. "It's this way, okay? I'm nuts for you. I can't stop thinking about you. I keep trying to forget you but it's not working. I broke up with Danny—or, I mean, Danny broke up with me. Because of you, because of...us. Because he saw us together Monday and he *knew*. He's the best guy I've ever known, he's the kind of guy I'd always dreamed about. And now he's gone. Because of you."

All this sounded pretty damn good to Fletcher—well, except for the part about the blue-collar boyfriend being so damn special. He asked wryly, "This is a problem?"

"Oh, very funny—and just tell me this. Tell me now. Have you got someone else, someone who loves you and thinks it's just you and her?"

"Absolutely not."

She blinked. "Well. That's *something*, I guess."

"Cleo, there's no one."

Her sweet lower lip quivered. She bit it to make it stop. "You know, even your sisters-in-law aren't so sure about you—well, except for Celia. She told me to go for it. To take action. And look at me now. I guess that's just what I *am* doing."

"Action is good. Action is exactly right."

"Oh, well. Yeah. You would say that."

"You've been talking to Celia—and Jillian and Jane?"

"Yes, I have. We did lunch. Just now, as a matter of fact, up at Celia's place. There was a very nice Chenin Blanc and I bawled my silly eyes out and told them *everything*. What do you think about that?"

He thought he wanted to touch her—everywhere. Now. But they were standing in a public hallway. A couple of plump tourists—a man and a woman in matching blue plaid shirts and khaki pants—had paused near the wall to take in the show. And a maid had stopped to watch, too. Fletcher only had to flick a glance at the maid and she scuttled off down the hall. The tourists, however, stayed right where they were. And there were others, strangers and one or two of his employees, striding past, not pausing but giving them way-too-interested glances as they went.

Cleo noticed their audience, too. "People are staring, you know that? We're making a spectacle, you and me."

Enough of this. He grabbed her hand. "Come on."

Wouldn't you know it? She dug in her heels. "To where?"

"My apartment."

"I don't know if that's a good idea. And don't you have some meeting you just have to go to?"

"Nothing that can't be rescheduled."

"Well, this is pretty sudden, and I'm not sure if we should just—"

He moved in a little closer. A hot burst of something that might have been triumph blasted through him when she didn't cringe away. He pitched his voice low. "Cleo, it's not the least sudden. We've been moving toward this for a month, since that first meeting in my office, and I have counted every damn endless day. It's too late to back out now. You've made your move. Now it's *my* move. Will you please let me make it?"

She shut her eyes, shook her head. And then her eyelids popped open and she glared straight at him. "Tell me this isn't really happening."

"I can't tell you that. Because—at last—it is."

He led her along one hallway and then another, holding tight to her hand, pulling her onward, giving her no chance to stop and think it over, no chance to change her mind.

Cleo didn't object. What was the use? In spite of all her doubts, she wanted this, she burned for it. Her blood sang through her veins and her belly felt hot and hollowed-out, hungry for the pleasure she knew he would bring her. She followed along, letting him lead her, until they reached the bank of elevators that included the one to his penthouse. He ushered her in ahead of him.

She went, in a sort of walking swoon of surrender. Once the car was swooping upward, he took out his cell phone and auto-dialed a number. "Marla," he said. "Reschedule with Thacker. Cancel my five o'clock. I'll reschedule that myself later...Yes...No." He disconnected the call and instantly made another. "Celia?" Oh, God.

"Yes. That's right. It's Fletcher. I'm with Cleo...Exactly. Will you pick up Ashlyn from preschool and keep her with you for a while?" And what was going to happen for *a while?* As if she didn't know... "Thanks...Yes. I'll pick her up by six." He flipped the phone shut and slid it back into the inside pocket of his suit coat.

By then, they had reached the penthouse floor. The doors whooshed open. Fletcher took her arm again. The contact—the absolute command in his touch—made her knees go to jelly. They stepped out into the hallway side by side. She tried not to cling to him, not to sway against him on her wobbly legs. She tried to show a little pride in this...total sexual capitulation, for crying out loud. Light from the skylight above made the gorgeous inlaid floor beneath their feet seem to glow.

He punched a code into the box by the wide doors to his suite and then he led her into the foyer, where a pleasant-faced middle-aged woman greeted them.

"You won't have to pick up Ashlyn, Mrs. Dolby," Fletcher told her. "Celia will take her for a few hours."

"Good enough, Mr. Bravo." With a sweet smile, she turned and left them.

Fletcher still had her arm. "This way." He guided her to the right, past the kitchen and the dining room and the family room where she had first met his daughter.

It seemed years ago somehow, that other day he'd brought her up here, the day she'd said yes to his plans for KinderWay. Forever ago. When she had still been able to tell herself that what was happening right now *wouldn't* happen, when she still believed that she would stay with Danny, that he was the right man for her.

She had no such illusions now. Now she understood that this attraction between her and Fletcher was too powerful to deny. It was exactly what she *hadn't* been looking for, but it was also something she could no longer escape.

He released her arm—but caught her hand instead. They went through a door, which he paused to close and lock behind them: his bedroom, the master suite. He went on, tugging her behind him, past the sitting area where the fat chairs and the sofa were of wonderfully soft-looking caramel-colored leather scattered about with pillows of tan and sage-green.

The bed was wide, with a sage-green spread and piles of gray and ivory pillows against a wide curving headboard of some grainless light-colored wood. He stopped right beside it and pulled her around so that she faced him.

"I want you. Now. Here."

Her body thrummed with excitement, with heat and desire. Already she could feel wetness between her legs.

"I've waited," he said. "I won't wait anymore." She only stared at him, at his lean face and his burning pale eyes. "Cleo," he said. It was a command.

And somehow from her clutching throat she got the necessary words out. "Yes. All right. Now."

Chapter Eight

Cleo lay on oyster-gray silk sheets.

She turned her head toward the bedside chair in the corner. Her clothes were laid out on it: her conservative knee-length silk dress of vivid royal blue, her bra, her panty hose, her white leather bag. In front of the chair, standing neatly side by side, were her camel suede pumps.

It was true. It was *real.* Her clothes were over there. And she was here.

In Fletcher's bed. Naked.

He rose up above her, naked as she was, all lean muscle and hard, hot flesh—and glowing wolf eyes. He braced himself on his fists. "Cleo," he said. "At last…"

And then, oh-so-slowly, he lowered himself down to her.

She couldn't stop herself; she moaned as his lips touched hers.

Unbelievable. Their first kiss—with both of them naked, their bodies pressed close. She wrapped her arms around those wide shoulders, her fingers slipping upward into his thick, silky hair. She breathed in and she breathed *him*—the expensive aftershave, the healthy male scent of his skin.

His mouth moved on hers, his tongue seeking, parting. With another low moan, she opened for him. His hot tongue swept her mouth, burning where it touched, and his body moved above hers slowly in one long, all-over caress.

She could feel him acutely—all of him. There, at the place where her thighs joined, he was thick and hard, nestled and nudging against her. He moved his hips, a slight, slow rocking. She rocked with him, holding him close, loving the way he felt, the way that their bodies fit so perfectly together, as if they'd been made to make love with each other.

He broke the burning kiss and he looked down at her, the blue rims around his irises darker than before, his fine mouth swollen from plundering hers. "Everything," he whispered. "Everything, all of you…"

And all she could say was, "Yes," and "Yes," again.

He eased his legs between hers, pushed up to his knees and loomed above her. She cried out at the loss of his fine, strong body on hers. And then she looked up at him and...

He was so thrilling to look at—wide shoulders, lean arms. A light dusting of silky dark hair formed a cross on that hard chest, nipple to nipple and trailing down in an enticing line over his corrugated belly. The lean, taut muscles of his thighs were temptingly prominent. From the nest of dark hair between those thighs, his erection jutted, stiff and ready for her.

His gaze was on her, moving, those eyes pale and shining as moons in the dark of night. "So beautiful," he whispered. "More beautiful than I imagined. And I did imagine. Often..."

He bent close again. And he began to kiss her—all over. She heard the hungry pleading noises coming from her own throat as he laid a knowing hand over the curls that covered her sex.

He sought and found the swollen secret flesh where her pleasure was greatest. With his thumb he teased that spot as his fingers delved lower, between the slick folds.

She cried out again at the searing delight he brought her, a cry he took into himself as he once more covered her mouth with his.

Her mind was on fire, like her body. She was liquid and she was fire, both at once. She was thoughtless, needful flesh and all she knew was the searing wet heat of his tongue in her mouth, the knowing way his fingers played her below.

He didn't rush. Oh, no. He took his time. He had the

slow hands women whisper of, the erotic skill to make her burn for the feel of him inside her.

More than once she tugged at him, moaning, urging him to fill her—but he wouldn't. He only kissed her some more and touched her yet more deeply.

Until she gave in. Until she couldn't hold out, couldn't wait. She felt her body rising, gathering, reaching the crest.

And then she went over with another sharp, shattered cry. Sweat dewed her body. She went limp with satisfaction. Sighing in contentment, she pushed his hand away.

But he wouldn't let her rest. His fingers, wet with the evidence of her desire, played along her rib cage, traced teasing patterns on her stomach. He tormented her with pleasure, arousing her all over again.

He stroked her thighs, took her breasts in each hand, covering one with his mouth, teasing her nipple between his teeth, worrying it and then latching on and sucking, drawing the yearning into a shining thread, a strand of pure heat spinning out and pulling tight from her breast to her womb.

And in no time she was crying out all over again, rising to meet him, all yearning and open and hungry for more.

It was then, deep within the delicious web of pleasure he wove so expertly around her, that she found herself remembering her mother, remembering Lolita, scenting again the smell of perfume and sex; seeing in her mind's eye the flushed, loose, dewy smile on her mother's beautiful face when she would come home from the first night with a new man.

These were powerful memories, old images that had always brought Cleo pain and bewilderment that her mother could be such a fool, could surrender to the same temptations over and over again.

Now, though, Cleo smiled between moans.

Incredible, but while Fletcher touched her, while his hands worked their thrilling magic on her flesh, in the heat and the wonder of this, she understood…

Everything.

She understood her mother for the very first time, understood how a woman might be willing to give up so much for the shining, hot joy of this; saw why Lolita had always chosen to toss herself, heedless of old lessons learned, into the arms of yet another player who could sweep her away like this.

Again Cleo rose to the peak, clutching the silk sheets, moaning his name, whispering, pleading, "Oh, please. Make it now…."

He kissed her so deeply and then he reached for the drawer in the bedside table, brought out a condom, tore the wrapping open and expertly slid it down over himself.

She watched him as he performed those necessary actions. She was achingly eager for the moment when he would slip between her thighs—and also reminded again that he was so good at this, that he must have had lots of practice.

But then, that wasn't news. She had known from the first he would be skilled at lovemaking. After all, there had been others before her, a glittering string of them, beautiful women every one of them, she had no doubt. Practice makes perfect, as they say.

How many of those women had really loved him? And how many only hungered for the pleasure he could give them, for the prestige having him at their side could bring them?

How many of them had Fletcher loved? If any…

Doesn't matter, she decided, gazing up him longingly. She was here now, naked, in his bed. Too late to wonder about the ones who came before her, too late to do anything but go where this magic took her.

His gray gaze was on her again. He held her eyes as he settled himself in place. She was way beyond ready, so wet and eager and open that he glided in all the way with the first thrust.

They both moaned.

And then she grabbed for him, pulling him fully down upon her, lifting and wrapping her legs around him, pressing her heels hard against him, urging him on.

He didn't need encouragement.

He moved, slow and long and deep at first, then gathering speed, stoking the fires within until the world spun away and there was only white-hot pleasure expanding out from the center of her, sweeping through her whole body, carrying her up and sending her over in a shower of endless, shimmering light.

Chapter Nine

"Come with me," he said, when six o'clock approached and with it the time to go to Celia's and pick up Ashlyn.

Cleo gazed up at him from her nest of silk-covered pillows and told him regretfully, "Oh, Fletcher. No. Not tonight…"

He bent his head and kissed her, hard and quick. "Why not?"

Naturally he *would* choose the question she didn't really know how to answer. Gamely she gave it a try. "I need a little time to myself, that's all. Time to think."

He was shaking his head. "Bad idea."

She frowned up at him. "What? Thinking?"

"Yeah, thinking—or more specifically overthinking.

You'll go home and you'll start stewing and before you know it—" he cupped her bare breast, flicked it with his tongue, bringing a pleasured gasp from her, before he lifted his dark head again, met her eyes and finished "—you'll have yourself convinced that this afternoon was a bad idea."

"No, I won't."

It was only half a lie. The sex had been fantastic. She didn't have it in her to call such delight a bad idea. But as far as the rest of it, as far as getting involved with this particular man...

It hadn't been wise. Not wise, not prudent. Not the least bit sensible.

And then again, maybe they weren't really involved. She might as well be a realist about this. A player is a player, and this afternoon could very well be not only the beginning but also the end of it.

He said, "You'll miss dinner with Ashlyn. I believe there will be Tater Tots."

She almost smiled. Really, if today was going to be all of it, he'd hardly be urging her to stick around and share the evening meal with him and his daughter. "It's tempting, but no."

He didn't argue further. He was smarter than that. What he did was kiss her—a wet, seeking kiss, a kiss hot with the promise of more pleasure to come. Then he threw back the covers and strode, naked and utterly amazing to look at, toward the open door to the bathroom, where he paused and turned back to her. "Come on."

She sat up and eyed him sideways. "To do what?"

"You are the most suspicious woman—to take a shower."

"Together?"

"That would be nice."

Nice was hardly the word for it, and he knew it, too. Those smoke-and-silver eyes promised a lot more than "nice." A flush of arousal swept through her as she imagined the two of them sharing a hot, steamy, leisurely shower, as she pictured soap bubbles sliding down his beautiful chest....

No way. Couldn't happen. If they fooled around in the shower, he'd never make it to Celia's apartment by six.

And she did need to go home, to recoup and reevaluate.

He must have read her thoughts in her expression, because he added, "Don't worry. There are two showers. You can lather up alone."

When they were both fully dressed again, he pulled her into his arms.

He kissed her. At length.

When he lifted his head, he commanded in a low tone, "Don't talk yourself out of this. Please..."

He looked...vulnerable. At that moment she was certain he'd be hurt if she refused to see him again. In spite of her strong reservations, her heart warmed to him. She could almost hope...

What? She wasn't quite sure. Maybe for more of

him than his gorgeous body. For his deepest secrets, that he might give them to her, to share. For his trust...

She told him honestly, "If I could talk myself out of this, I would have done it already."

"But you couldn't—you can't."

"I don't think so. Especially not after today..."

He traced the line of her jaw, his touch setting off sparks. "Now that's what I like to hear."

Going home didn't help much. The cozy rooms seemed kind of empty and she felt at a loss—for Fletcher. How crazy was that?

She sat on her sofa and pretended to watch the news and relived every moment of the afternoon before— every sigh, every kiss, every lingering touch.

The phone rang at nine and she knew it would be him.

"Hello?"

"I hope to hell you're not thinking."

Happiness glowed all through her. Was she foolish? Oh, yes. Did she care?

Not hardly. "I *have* been thinking, as a matter of fact. Thinking about this afternoon..."

"I love it when you get that husky tone. I know then that I've got you."

"As always, you are stunningly sure of yourself."

Was he smiling? Oh, yes. She knew that he was. "I'm going to consider that a compliment," he said.

"Ah," she said, because the truth was, her mind was

so filled with him, there was no room left for thinking up clever replies.

"I wish you were here with me."

She found, incredibly, that she believed him. "I'm glad," she answered softly.

"What are you wearing?"

She threw back her head and she laughed, then she whispered into the mouthpiece, "Who *is* this?"

"A very bad man. Tell me what you're wearing."

She sighed—good and loud, so he would be sure to hear it. "I'll say this much, I'm looking really glamorous."

"I want specifics."

"Don't go there. Keep your illusions."

"I said specifics."

"You'll be sorry."

"I'll be the judge of that."

"Just remember, you asked for it. I'm wearing ugly old sweatpants."

"Sweatpants excite me. What color?"

"Oh, come on…"

"What color?"

She gave in and told him. "Light blue."

"Sexy."

"If you say so…"

"I do. What else?"

"A stretched out KinderWay T-shirt and ratty slippers."

"I'm getting that feeling. You know which one I mean?"

"I could guess…."

"And underneath the blue sweatpants?"

"Panties. Plain cotton."

"White?"

"Yes."

"I love plain white cotton. So…functional."

"Well, yes. It's that."

"Bra?"

"I'll never tell."

"Take it all off. Now."

"Fletcher?"

"What?"

"Is this phone sex we're having?"

"Now you're catchin' on."

The next morning, Friday, she was in the five-year-olds' room when he dropped Ashlyn off.

"Cleo!" Ashlyn ran to her.

She bent down and caught the warm little body close in her arms. "Oh, it's so good to see you."

Ashlyn pulled back and laid her small, soft hand so briefly against Cleo's cheek. It felt absolutely lovely, that fond, trusting touch. The little girl asked, "Can I read to you today?"

"I would like that very much."

"When?"

"How about morning playtime? I'll come back here to your classroom."

"Don't forget."

"I won't. I promise." She rose to her height again,

a delicious flush sweeping through her as she met Fletcher's eyes.

"Walk me out to the gate," he said.

She joined him as he turned for the door.

Once out of the classroom, they crossed the breezeway and headed down the walk. At the gate he paused and turned to her. "Tonight?"

Her heart beat in a lazy, deep kind of way. Her blood moved slow and sweet through her veins as she thought of the afternoon before—of last night on the phone. "Yes."

"I'll pick you up at eight."

He arrived right on time. They went to a little Italian place he knew off the Strip, away from the glitz and the glitter. The food was good and the wine even better.

She held it to one glass. Just being with him was challenge enough to her good sense. He asked her about her years as a showgirl and she told him everything he wanted to know—about the shows she'd been in and the killing hours, working all night, going to school in the daytime.

"It was tough. I never got enough sleep. After a show, we'd all be keyed up. The temptation was to hang out with the other dancers, have a few drinks, kind of come down. But when I did that, I wouldn't get to bed until after daylight. In my case, I needed to be at my first class at ten. No way. I had to force myself to go straight home."

"You have discipline."

She laughed. "There's not a professional dancer in the world who doesn't have an excess of that. The work is so demanding. And you just can't fake it. But for me, well, I was after a different kind of life. And I was fortunate. I managed to take what I knew—dancing—and use it to get where I wanted to go."

She asked about how he had gotten where he was now. He told her how he had come up through the casinos in Atlantic City.

"Dealer, floor supervisor, pit boss, assistant shift manager—you name the job, I've probably done it. The irony is, while I was learning the business in New Jersey, Aaron was doing the same thing here in Nevada. We knew *of* each other, had even met briefly—twice—before we learned that we were brothers."

"You're kidding. You met, realized you had the same last name—and you didn't even wonder if you might be related?"

"Bravo's not *that* uncommon a name."

"But you look a lot alike…"

He shrugged those wide shoulders. "What can I tell you? The truth was right there in front of us, we just didn't see it. But then Jonas and Aaron formed the Bravo Group. They were looking for someone to run Impresario. They had me checked out before they approached me and in the process discovered who my father was. It all pretty much fell into place from there."

"And that was when?"

"I moved here two years ago."

"Was Ashlyn living with you then?"

He shook his head. "Her mother was still alive.

Belinda died a few months after I came to Vegas."
Belinda. His ex was named Belinda.

"That must have been hard," said Cleo. "For Ashlyn,
especially. To lose her mother so young…"

He watched her. She thought he seemed…wary
somehow. Then he looked down. "Kids are resilient."

"So people always say."

He glanced up again, a sharp gleam in his eye. "You
think they're not?"

"I think children are tender and open and defenseless.
They can be easily damaged. And I think it's nothing
short of a miracle what some kids live through and yet
still manage to lead happy, productive lives." She
reached across the table and touched his arm. When he
looked at her once more, she added, "And I also think
Ashlyn is really something. I think you—and her mother—have done a great job with her. She's not only bright
and beautiful, she's fun in her own oh-so-serious way
and she's interested in others. She's a terrific kid."

He gave her a slow nod. "Thank you."

"Hey. It's only the truth. Was Belinda sick?"

He glanced away, then back. "Her death was sudden."

"And when she died, you two had been divorced
for…?"

Something had definitely happened in his eyes—
something final, like a thick door swinging shut. "About
three years."

Cleo did the math. "You mean, you were divorced
before Ashlyn was born?"

A pause. He sipped his wine, set the glass down, then gave out grudgingly, "The divorce was final a few months *after* she was born."

"So…you broke up while your wife was pregnant with Ashlyn?"

"That's right—how about dessert?"

"No thanks." She fiddled with her water glass. "You don't want to talk about her, about your ex-wife…."

He looked at her steadily now. "No, I don't. There's no point. All that's in the past." And then he reached across the white tablecloth and laid his hand over hers. "The tiramisu is excellent here."

"No. Really. No more."

"Shall we go, then?"

"All right." She saw promises in his eyes, erotic ones. Her curiosity about the lost Belinda faded—for the moment anyway. She was all breathlessness, all yearning desire.

He took care of the check and they were out of there. In the car he glanced over at her. "Come home with me."

Oh, how she wanted to do just that. But she was having another dose of second thoughts, thinking again how she couldn't afford to get too wrapped up in him. "I don't know. It's getting kind of late."

"A lame excuse if I ever heard one. It's barely ten and it's Friday. No KinderWay tomorrow."

He was right. And besides, she couldn't bear to say good-night. Not yet. She suggested, "You could come to my place…."

"Why? So you can kick me out as soon as you've gotten what you want from me?"

She felt the grin as it tugged at the corners of her mouth. "I would never do that."

"Good to know—but I have plans."

"And they are?"

"We can stop by your house. You can pick up what you need for tomorrow. We'll spend the day together—you and me and Ashlyn."

"You want me to stay the night at your place, you mean?"

"Yes. I do."

It seemed…shocking somehow, that he would suggest she spend a whole night in his bed. She wasn't quite sure why. Maybe because of Ashlyn. The day before, he'd been so careful to make sure that Ashlyn was nowhere around while they made love. "Has Ashlyn gone somewhere for the night, then?"

He took his gaze off the road long enough to send her a puzzled glance. "No. Why?"

"Well, if I stayed at your apartment, Ashlyn would find me there in the morning."

Even in profile his amusement was clear. "Gee whiz. You're right."

"I'm serious. I just don't…" The words trailed off as she tried to figure out how to finish.

"You don't what?"

"Oh, I don't know. Will that bother her if she finds me there in the morning?"

"Cleo, you've taken child-development classes. You know how a five-year-old thinks. Ashlyn likes you. A lot. If you show up at the breakfast table, she's only going to think that you're there to see *her.*" He sent her another glance and his voice went to velvet. "And I promise not to do X-rated things to you unless we're alone in my bedroom with the door locked." He looked at the road again. "Say yes. Say it now."

She shouldn't. And she knew it. But she said it anyway. "Yes."

Much later, as they lay in his bed, drowsy and contented and thoroughly satisfied, he asked her if she was on the pill.

She told him no. She hadn't liked the side effects. "I do have a diaphragm…."

He smoothed her hair off her forehead and placed a kiss at her temple. "Whatever. Just wondered. I don't mind using condoms—if you don't."

"Condoms are fine with me." She rolled so she was on her side, facing him, and snuggled in closer. Funny. Even the mundane and often awkward contraception conversation seemed somehow perfectly natural and easy with Fletcher.

Maybe because he's had that particular conversation so many times…

The snide thought came into her mind and she ordered it away. It wouldn't quite go. "Fletcher?" He made a low sound, one that told her he was listening.

She laid a hand on his hard chest, felt the slow, strong beating of his heart beneath her palm. "Maybe you'll think I'm backward and conservative. But I do work with kids. It's part of my job to be…more respectable than most."

"Meaning?"

"Well, it could be considered suspect. You're funding my preschool and here I am in your bed."

"It's no one's business," he said. "No one's business but ours. And I'm not going to sneak around if that's what you're asking for."

She realized she wasn't. Not really. "I just want you to understand. This isn't…casual for me."

He tipped her chin up to him. "And you assume that it is for me?"

"I assume nothing." It wasn't true. She *had* made assumptions. And she probably shouldn't have. She tried a different tack. "Let me put it this way. For as long as it lasts between us…"

She felt his lips in her hair, the warmth of his breath as he kissed the crown of her head. "Say it," he whispered.

"I want faithfulness from you. I want for there to be no other women, only me." He was quiet. But he did run a finger up the side of her arm, causing warm little shivers to bloom beneath her skin. She tipped her head back so she could see his face. "Well?"

His eyes burned into hers. "Do I get the same from you?"

"You do." She told him the truth. "As a matter of fact, I've been faithful to you since the day that I met you." Something flared in his eyes. Triumph? Possessiveness? She wasn't sure. She added, "I spent several weeks denying it, trying to keep from admitting to myself that the only man I wanted touching me was you. But I've... faced up to it now."

"Brave of you."

"I think so."

"And will you *stay* faithful to me—for as long as we're together?"

Piece-of-cake question. "Yes. Absolutely."

"Fair enough, then. It's a deal."

And he kissed her, gently at first and then more deeply. The world centered down to his hands on her flesh, his knowing mouth and his wicked tongue. She could much too easily grow accustomed to spending her nights in Fletcher's bed.

The next morning Ashlyn behaved as Fletcher had predicted.

Her face lit up when Cleo entered the kitchen. "Cleo! You came to my house. I'm so glad."

They shared a leisurely breakfast, the three of them. Ashlyn chattered away about how much she liked her school, about her friends, about the story she was "writing."

"It's called *The Happy Ladybug*. It's mostly pictures. I have a very large vocabulary." She pronounced the big word with obvious pride. "I mean, for a five-year-old, but I can't spell all those words yet."

As Mrs. Dolby began clearing off, Fletcher put his hand over Cleo's. She reveled in the warmth of his touch. Then he said, "Okay. Time for a confession."

"Should I be worried?"

"The truth is, I've got to work for a few hours."

She frowned. "Now?"

He looked so charmingly guilty. "Here's the truth. I was afraid if I told you earlier, you'd leave."

Ashlyn piped right up. "But you can't leave, Cleo. You have to see my book. The happy ladybug is hiding from a big, fat robin. She's very scared. We have to figure out how to save her. And as soon as she's safe from danger, then we can play some games."

Fletcher's lean hand tightened over hers. "Please stay. I won't be too long…."

So Cleo and Ashlyn retired to the family room, where Ashlyn brought out her work in progress and they discussed ways the ladybug might keep from being the robin's lunch.

Then they got down on the floor to play Concentration. Ashlyn was amazingly adept at the game. If she turned over a card, she remembered it.

"My uncle Cade taught me," she explained. "Uncle Cade is married to Aunt Jane."

"That's right. I remember."

"He's a gambler, Uncle Cade is. That's his job. You would like Uncle Cade, Cleo. He's almost as handsome as Daddy. And whenever I see him, he picks me up and swings me high in the air and he calls me Princess. He says that I can remember cards because it runs in the family."

There were only ten cards left on the floor when Cleo's purse started playing the William Tell Overture. She took out her cell phone and saw that the caller was Celia.

"Just checking on you," her new friend said. "I had to make sure that Fletcher is treating you right."

Cleo grinned and pitched her voice low enough that Ashlyn, still on the floor with the cards, wouldn't hear. "You are dying to know what happened—in detail."

"Bust-ed. Listen, can you talk?"

Ashlyn glanced up then.

Cleo met those wide, watchful eyes. "Well, as a matter of fact, Ashlyn was just beating the pants off me at Concentration."

"You're at Fletcher's."

"I am."

"And he has to work."

"How did you know?"

"I'm married to his brother. Come on over, both you and Ashlyn. It's just me and the kids—until noon, when Aaron has sworn to join us for a little quality family time."

"But Fletcher said he'd be finished in an hour or so."

"Cleo, it doesn't matter what he said. Take it from a woman with a Bravo man of her own. He won't be finished until noon. And if he is, Mrs. Dolby can tell him where to find you."

* * *

At Celia's, J.J. was napping. Ashlyn trotted right off to Davey's room. Cleo and Celia took seats on a sofa in the living room.

"You know," said Celia once Cleo had brought her up to date on the Fletcher situation, "he *has* had a few girlfriends in the past couple of years…."

"Is that supposed to reassure me?"

"Let me finish. He's had girlfriends—but until you, none of them have gotten anywhere near Ashlyn."

"So you think maybe he's looking for a new nanny?"

Celia leaned closer. Winter sunlight from the wall of windows behind them brought out the gold highlights in her red hair. "I'm serious. This is a major step for him. You're the only one he's allowed near his little girl. And look *how* near. He leaves you alone with her. That's a very big thing, believe me. He's so…protective of her. He works like a demon, but that child is the center of his life."

Cleo bit her lip and nodded. "I know that. I do. And…well, I have to admit I'm beginning to feel a little hopeful about the two of us. The past couple of days have been like a dream come true…."

Celia knew there was more. "But?"

Again Cleo kept it low. "Last night I asked him about his ex-wife. He was reluctant to talk about her—more than reluctant. It was like a curtain going down. Maybe it's too early for me to be asking him such hard questions."

Celia brushed her shoulder with a light hand. "I can

tell you this—it's not just you. That I know of, he rarely talks about her to anyone."

"You mean, at least I'm not alone?"

Celia looked sheepish. "Yeah. And I can tell you what *I* know...."

"Oh, please. Yes."

"Well..." Celia kicked off her flats, tucked her legs to the side and braced an elbow on the back of the sofa. "Aaron says they got married in college."

"They met there?"

"Uh-huh. At Princeton. He was studying finance on full scholarship. She was in humanities—English Lit, something like that. They both got their degrees. And he went into the casino business. I don't think she worked. The marriage lasted for five years or so. Then Belinda got pregnant with Ashlyn—and then the marriage broke up. He left her and he also gave her full custody of Ashlyn."

Cleo let out a hard breath. "You're not serious. He wouldn't do that—not the way he feels about his family, not the way he is with Ashlyn now."

Celia shrugged. "But he did do that. I remember when Ashlyn first came here to live with him. He never saw that little girl until Belinda's parents contacted him to tell him that his ex-wife had died."

"It seems...completely unlike him. He's tough and he can be scary, but I understood that first day I met him that to him family is everything. His *child* is everything. You even said so yourself." And Cleo was hungry for any information she could get. "How did Belinda die?"

"He didn't tell you?"

"He said it was 'sudden.'"

"It was. She had a stroke. One of those freak things you'd never imagine could happen to someone that young. She and Ashlyn were at Belinda's parents' house in upstate New York. Belinda told her mother she had a headache. She went to lie down—and never got back up again. Her mother went to check on her and found her dead."

"How awful…"

Celia touched her shoulder again. "It *is* very new between you and Fletcher. And he's been hurt. He's a guarded man—just like Aaron was when he and I got together. Fletcher never knew his father. He loves his step-father, but Grant didn't come along until later. I think Fletcher and his mother had a tough time there for a while."

"Grant. That's his stepfather's name?"

"Yeah. Grant Holland. He's a great guy. Truly. So Fletcher did get at least half of a decent childhood. But then there was Belinda. And whatever went wrong there, I'd guess the wounds go deep."

"I have to say I think you're right."

"But, Cleo…"

"What?"

Celia's hazel eyes twinkled. "I think it's all work-able—for the two of you."

"Oh, God. Not really. Not in any permanent way. He's just not the kind for that."

"Oh, yes he is. With the right woman, a woman like you…"

Cleo reminded herself not to float too far up in the clouds. She teased, "And you know this how?"

"Intuition."

"Oh. Well."

"Don't you dare scoff at intuition."

"I'm not scoffing. It's only, well, I'm hardly daring to believe the way this is going. The other day, when it started with us, I was absolutely certain Fletcher and I couldn't last five minutes."

"Yeah. You made your doubts painfully clear at lunch."

"Two big glasses of Chenin Blanc will do that to a girl."

"Oh, so now you say it was the wine...."

"Well, without it, you and Jane and Jilly would never know all my deepest secrets."

"Then here's to white wine—and serendipity. You shared your feelings about Fletcher and then you instantly ran into him."

"Was that strange or what?"

"Cleo, *life* is strange. And miracles do happen. They did for me. One day I realized I was in love with my boss—a guy I'd known all my life, a guy I knew would never look twice at me, what with the glamour girls he always dated. I thought it was hopeless. But look at me now. Happily married to the very man I was certain would never love me in return—and with two gorgeous kids, to boot."

"Oh, Celia, it's all happening so fast, you know? Here it is, three days later, and I'm finding myself hoping the craziest thing...."

"Tell," Celia commanded.

"It's too wild."

"Tell me anyway. I can take it."

"Well, okay, then. I'm starting to dare to imagine what it might be like if Fletcher and I had a lifetime." A nervous laugh escaped her. "Is that insane or what?"

"Not in the least."

"Well, it's nice that you sound so sure."

"I am sure. I am absolutely positive. I am a total romantic and darn proud of it. And you know what? I'm going to lay it right out here."

"Lay *what* right out here?"

"The truth as I see it."

"And that would be...?"

"Cleo, what I think we've got here is love."

Chapter Ten

Love.

Could it be?

Though Celia's enthusiasm was contagious, Cleo thought it was a little too early to be calling what she felt for Fletcher *love*. She wouldn't put labels on it. No. Not yet.

She'd just…go with it. See where this thing between them took her. He wasn't the man she saw herself building a life with—and yet, there was no way she could turn her back on the power of what she felt for him.

So she decided to enjoy herself, day-to-day.

For a woman like Cleo, who liked to know where she was going and how long it would take to get there, keeping it open-ended was a whole new approach. But she did it anyway. With enthusiasm.

She spent every spare moment at Fletcher's side and every night in his bed. Within a week she'd moved half her wardrobe over to his place. It was just easier, she reasoned, to use his penthouse as home base. They both had demanding jobs and there were only so many hours in a day. If she kept her things at his place, she didn't end up wasting precious time going back and forth to her house after work and in the early morning.

He gave her half of his huge walk-in closet and dressing room: endless hanger space, two sides of the big central chest of drawers and all she needed of the slanted cedar shelves built especially for shoes.

"Bring it all over," he suggested. "I've got plenty of room. And if it keeps you here with us longer, it works for me."

Us.

He meant Ashlyn, too. The three of them just naturally fell into a routine. Every morning they shared breakfast in the penthouse kitchen, then Cleo would take Ashlyn down to KinderWay. On the nights when Cleo and Fletcher didn't go out, they would all three have dinner together.

It was working out beautifully, Cleo thought. She was actually happy just taking it day-to-day. Fletcher and Ashlyn seemed happy, too.

No, Cleo didn't really believe that it would last forever. But while it did, well, she was certainly having the best time of her life.

The only faint shadow on her happiness was the mystery of the lost Belinda. Cleo still wanted to know what had happened in his marriage, what had gone so wrong that he had not only put his wife behind him, but also, for three years, his child.

She didn't raise the subject, though. Eventually, she was sure, if they stayed together long enough, they would get around to it again.

On Friday morning—a week and a day after she and Fletcher became lovers—as Cleo and Ashlyn walked along the hotel hallways headed for KinderWay, Ashlyn tugged on Cleo's hand. Cleo smiled down at her.

Ashlyn didn't smile back—but then, she rarely smiled. She said in an easy, conversational tone, "My mommy was tall, like you, Cleo. And so pretty. She died." Cleo slowed her steps a little as Ashlyn frowned, considering. "I don't remember her very well. I think she was nice. But until Daddy came to get me, I mostly stayed with Grandma and Grandpa."

Iron-lace benches with seats lushly padded in red and gold were spaced at intervals along the hallway. "Come on," Cleo said. "Let's sit down."

Ashlyn hung back. "But we have to go to my school."

"Just for a moment or two." She led the child to the nearest bench.

Ashlyn obediently climbed up and sat. "Okay." She waited until Cleo was seated, too, then folded her hands in her lap. "We're sitting."

Cleo looked at the sweet upturned face of Fletcher's child and felt distinctly devious. Trying to get his daughter to tell her the things Fletcher hadn't said himself…

How low was that?

But then again, maybe this was a subject Ashlyn needed to explore. She asked gently, "Do you want to talk about your mother?"

Ashlyn wrinkled up her pert nose. "Well, no. I mostly want to go to my school right now."

So much for Ashlyn's burning need to confide. "You know what?" said Cleo. "You're right. We should get to school."

"O-*kay*." Ashlyn jumped eagerly to her feet. "Let's go." She reached for Cleo's hand again and they proceeded down the hallway toward the bank of French doors that led outside and to KinderWay. A few steps along, she looked up again. "Cleo?"

"Hmm?"

"Where's *your* mommy?"

"She died, too, but it was after I was all grown up."

"Do you miss her?"

"Yes, I do."

"What about your daddy?"

"He's still alive. I don't see him very often, though."

"Tell him to come to my house. I'll read him a story. He'll like that."

Cleo pushed open the door and they went through into the misty, cool February morning. "We'll see."

* * *

That night in bed, after sweet, slow lovemaking, Cleo told Fletcher what Ashlyn had said about Belinda.

She felt the movement of his shoulder as he shrugged. "They're good people, Belinda's folks. And they dote on Ashlyn. She went back for long visits twice last year. And she'll stay with them again this spring for a week or so."

"Stay with them where?"

"Bridgewater, New Jersey. It's about twenty miles north of Princeton. Belinda grew up there—and she moved back when we separated."

"But I hadn't realized Ashlyn lived with her grandparents while Belinda was alive. I thought—"

"Cleo, it's not a huge mystery. She was a single mother and her parents looked after Ashlyn so she could work."

"Belinda worked?"

Fletcher canted up on an elbow and looked down at her. "What? That surprises you? *You* work."

"Well, Celia mentioned that she didn't think Belinda had a job while you were married…."

The recessed lights in the bedroom were turned low, casting his face into shadow. Still, she couldn't miss the flash of his white teeth as he grinned. "Celia just *happened* to mention that, huh?"

"Okay, I asked. And yes, I'm curious about what went wrong between you and Belinda."

He touched her cheek, traced the line of her hair

where it fell against the side of her throat. "What do you want to know?" He sounded—what?—resigned maybe.

Still, her heart lifted. Whatever his attitude, he *was* willing to talk. "Oh, only everything…" She laid her palm against his warm chest and felt the low chuckle as it rumbled through him.

"Belinda got a job in some clothing store, I think. She left Ashlyn with her mother pretty much round-the-clock. She would stay with them on the weekends."

"Belinda was close to her parents, then?"

"Very—and why don't you go ahead and fill me in on what Celia just *happened* to tell you."

"Be glad to." She repeated all that Celia had said.

When she was done, he was quiet for a moment. Then he nodded. "Yeah. Belinda died of a stroke. It was a complete shock to everyone…."

She laid her hand on the side of his face. "Fletcher?"

He bent close enough to kiss the tip of her nose. "Why do I sense more questions coming?"

"Maybe because you're a very smart man."

There was a moment. She had a feeling he would tell her that they'd talked of this enough. But then he said, "All right. Fire away."

She did exactly that. "What happened…between you two? Why did you end up divorced?"

He caught her wrist, gently opened her fingers and placed a warm kiss in the heart of her palm. Then he pressed her hand to his chest again. "Belinda hated Atlantic City. She didn't like the gaming industry and she missed her hometown. And I was working killing hours—even more so than now, if that's possible—trying to establish myself and move up. She felt…deserted by me, I guess you could say. I didn't understand why she couldn't try harder to fit into my world. And it really got to me that she would resent my working hard when, in the end, I was working for us, for our future.

"By the last year we were married, she was spending more time in Bridgewater than with me. She told me she was pregnant and that she wanted a divorce in pretty much the same sentence. She also wanted full custody. I gave her everything she asked for—alimony and child support *and* sole custody of the baby. All of it. I was bitter. I felt she hadn't tried hard enough to make things work. I threw money at her and told myself I was glad to be rid of her."

"But…what about Ashlyn?"

"You want the hard truth?"

"Please."

"I didn't think a whole lot about her. My accountant sent the money and I went on with my climb up the gaming-business ladder—and you don't approve, do you? I can see it in the way you're pointing your chin at me."

"No, Fletcher. I don't approve."

"Neither do I. Now. But the ugly truth is, until Belinda died and I met Ashlyn for the first time, she just wasn't *real* to me."

"How sad—for her. *And* for you."

"I couldn't agree more."

"But I'm glad that at least you and your daughter finally…found each other. And that you have a good relationship with Belinda's parents. That's important, I think, for her to know her mother's side of the family."

"I think so, too. Any more questions?"

"Not right at the moment."

"Don't hesitate. Anytime you're the least bit curious, ask away."

"Oh, don't you worry. I definitely will." As she looked up through the shadows into his pale eyes, she felt she knew enough now about what had ended his marriage to Belinda that this particular part of Fletcher's past wouldn't nag at her mind so much. "And thank you."

"For…?"

"Helping me to understand."

"I live to serve."

"Well, I wouldn't go *that* far."

"Cleo?"

"Hmm?"

"Kiss me."

"Great idea." She smiled and lifted her mouth to his.

Friday, she and Fletcher planned to have lunch at Club Rouge, but he called at the last minute to say his meeting was running late.

"I'll make it up to you," he promised, his voice low and intimate, causing shivers to skitter along her skin. "Tonight…"

Cleo settled for a sandwich at one of the sidewalk

cafés along the indoor boulevard between the casino and Hotel Impresario. She'd just placed her order for a BLT and a large iced tea when a feminine voice said, "Cleo Bliss. It's been a while."

She looked up. "Andrea. How are you?"

"Oh, you know…" The showgirl slid into the seat across from her. "Workin'. I've got a featured part in *Cancan du Bal*."

"Hey. That's good news, huh?"

"I'm doing okay." The waitress trotted back over bearing a menu. Andrea waved it away. "Brush-up rehearsal in ten minutes. You know how it goes…."

"I remember. Yes."

Andrea flipped a swatch of thick dark hair back over her shoulder and recrossed her long denim-clad legs. Cleo had done two shows with Andrea, a rock revue over at the Luxor and a rip-off of *Cats* at one of the smaller resorts. They'd always gotten along well enough, though they'd never been what you'd call friends.

"So," said Andrea. "I heard you did it. You're living your big dream. You opened a day care."

"A preschool. Yes, I did."

"And now you've opened one here, too, at Impresario."

The waitress set Cleo's iced tea at her elbow. She picked it up and sipped from it. "Word gets around."

"That's right. All those nights of going home early, missing the party, paid off for you, I guess." Cleo made a sound in her throat, the kind that might have meant anything. Andrea folded her forearms on the table. The diamond bracelet on her right arm caught the light, giving off a glitter as hard and bright as the one in her sapphire-blue eyes. She pitched her voice low. "I hear you're with Fletcher now."

Fletcher. First name only. Cleo got the message. Loud and much too clear. "Yes, I am." She sipped more tea.

"Like you said a minute ago, word gets around. You know how it is."

"Oh, yes. I know."

"He's a driven man, Fletcher is." Andrea pretended to fan herself. "What a body, huh? Somehow he makes time for the gym five days a week. I like a man with cheese-grater abs—hey, nice watch."

"Thank you. Beautiful bracelet."

Andrea held up her wrist, flicked it back and forth so the diamonds twinkled wildly. "I love it. 'Square cut or pear-shaped,' as the old song goes."

Cleo set down her glass. "Andrea."

"Yeah."

"Was there something specific you wanted to say to me?"

The dancer stopped flicking her bracelet and waved her hand instead. "Oh, only that nothing lasts forever, I guess. That some men just aren't the forever type. They like to go after you, they like to love you up. And they're good at it. They make you burn. But once you're caught, it can get old really fast for them. Am I making any sense?"

"Perfect sense. Is that all, then?"

"Oh, yeah." Andrea's full lips quivered. "I guess it is." She bent her sleek dark head. When she looked up again, those stunning blue eyes glittered with unshed tears.

Cleo dug in her purse and brought out a tissue. "Here."

Andrea took it. "Thanks." She blotted her eyes. "Hey. What do you know? I think I'm jealous."

"Yeah," said Cleo softly. "It kind of looks that way."

"I thought I was past it, past *him*. But then I saw you sitting here, in your cute little short blazer, your geometric print skirt and business pumps and…" She sniffed, tossed her head. "God. F-O-O-L. That would be me."

Cleo resisted the urge to reach out to the other woman. She knew the gesture would only be rebuffed. "Let it go," she said quietly.

"Let what go?" Andrea demanded.

"This. Just now. Your stopping by this table to tell me all about Fletcher. Let it go."

"And you? Will you let it go, too?"

"Yes, I will."

Andrea squinted at her, as if trying to get inside her mind, to find out if Cleo really meant what she said. Then, at last, she shrugged and hitched her huge tote firmly onto her shoulder. "If you tell him I talked to you, you can probably get me fired." She rose.

"I won't do that."

"Whatever. Story of my life, either way." It was all

bravado and they both knew it. Andrea had let the green monster get the better of her for a minute. But she didn't want to lose a good job. "See you around. And don't worry. In spite of this little lapse I just had here, I do know the routine. Smile. Nod. And walk on by."

"Something wrong?" Fletcher asked that night as they lay in their favorite place—his bed.

Andrea Raye, she thought. *That's what's wrong.*

Which was silly. After all, it wasn't as if Andrea had told her anything she didn't already know. Fletcher liked women. He'd been with several—Andrea among them, apparently.

Oh, wow, big news.

He guided her chin around so she looked at him, at his handsome, lean face and into his unforgettable eyes. "You seem far away."

She considered telling him what Andrea had said. She could lay it on him and then get his word that he wouldn't take steps to get Andrea kicked off Cancan du Bal.

But she'd promised Andrea she wouldn't say anything. And she was just unsure enough of how Fletcher might react to feel uncomfortable jeopardizing another woman's job.

When it's over, it's over, Lolita used to say in the tough times, after another man had left her. *I like to play with the big boys, so I gotta know how to let it go when the game is at an end. I keep my head up and I don't complain. I move on, baby. That's how it works. Those are the rules.*

Andrea had broken the rules. Cleo couldn't bring herself to take the chance that the other woman might have to pay for that. A dancer's life was tough enough without getting canned for telling the truth to the CEO's current girlfriend.

And besides, Cleo couldn't help sympathizing with Andrea. She knew *she'd* probably be eaten up with jealousy, too, if it ever became *her* turn to move on....

If? taunted a voice in the back of her mind. Oh, please. *You mean when...*

Fletcher bent closer. She felt his warm breath across her cheek. He caught her lower lip between his teeth— so lightly—tugged and let it go. Then he whispered, his mouth against hers, "Hello? Are you in there?"

"I'm here."

"No. I don't think so. You are far, far away...."

She lifted her arms—lazily—and wrapped them around his neck. "Wrong. I'm right here."

"Prove it." Beneath the covers, his hand swept downward. She moaned. "Better," he whispered. "Let's try that again...."

Fletcher woke first the next morning. He rolled his head to look at the woman beside him.

Cleo lay on her stomach, her face turned toward the far wall, all that glorious auburn hair spilling across the gray silk pillow. Slowly, carefully, he peeled back the blankets that covered her, pushing them all the way down to the foot of the bed.

Then he stretched out beside her again and admired what he'd revealed—starting with the vulnerable pink soles of her long, slim feet, moving up over the shapely ankles, the muscular calves, that tender, pale curve at the back of her knee.

From there it only got better: the long, firm thighs, the round, muscular bottom, the inviting sacral dimples at the base of her spine that made him want to bend close, dip his tongue in one and then the other. The scent of her tempted him—sweet and just a little spicy.

Yeah, he'd always enjoyed beautiful women. But Cleo—she was one of a kind. She had it all: not only the drop-dead looks but also the brains and the pure will to succeed. Plus, she possessed that smoldering extra something: call it an inner confidence, a sense of feminine power. Whatever. It made the men sit up and stare.

Men wanted her—though they'd sure as hell better keep away unless they wanted to deal with *him*. And not only did men desire her, women *liked* her. She could conquer the world, just as her name promised, as her mother had wanted her to.

But Cleo wasn't interested in running the world.

She only wanted to make a place for kids to learn. To have a family…

Yeah. She was special. There was no one quite like her. He was long gone over her and perfectly content to be so. Not since those first magic months with Belinda had he felt quite the way he felt right now.

Belinda…

Uh-uh. No point in going there.

He'd messed up with Belinda. She'd been all wrong for him. Weak. Not focused. A woman from a nice middle-class family who didn't understand the first thing about his world.

A woman nothing like the one beside him right now.

He continued his slow, appreciative scrutiny, admiring the sleek curves of her back, the leanly muscled shape of her dancer's arms—one bent at the elbow supporting her head, the other resting along her side. He was just getting to the poetry in her slim, long-fingered hands when she stirred and yawned and rolled to her back.

"What?" She squinted up at him, her face sleep-flushed and so beautiful it hurt to look at her—hurt in a very good way.

"Just admiring the view…" He traced a finger around a pert, pink nipple.

She lightly slapped his hand away. "The *view* is getting chilly since you stole all my covers."

"Let me warm you up."

She smiled at him then. Damned if her smile couldn't light up the darkest night. "Hmm. You know, that's an excellent idea…."

And then, before he had a chance to take the lead, her warm, soft hand closed around him. The feel of her gripping him was so perfect, so exactly right, that a low, pleasured moan escaped him.

She was still smiling—a much naughtier smile than before. "How about…like this?"

"Oh, yeah…"

She put her other hand—the one that wasn't doing incredible things to his suddenly rock-hard erection—on his chest. Gently she pushed him over until he lay on his back. Then she canted up over him. That cinnamon hair brushed his chest. The scent of her swam around him. She whispered, "And like this…?"

He could only nod as those long fingers of hers stroked him, slow, knowing strokes.

How did she do it?

The woman drove him wild.

She worked him, milking him with her hand, and she kissed her way down the center of his chest. When she took him in her mouth, he was absolutely certain he was going to explode.

Somehow he managed to hold back as her soft lips closed over him, as the wet cave of her silky mouth surrounded him, sucking. He rolled his head on the pillow and groaned low in his throat and tried not to reach for her….

He could only hold out for so long. The moment came too quickly when he couldn't take the sweet sexual torture she inflicted for one second more.

So he caught her by the shoulders and pulled her up to face him.

"Hey." She grinned down at him. "I wasn't finished."

"Maybe not. But if you don't stop, I *will* be."

Her fingers tightened on him again. "Fine with me."

He groaned. "Wait." And then he swore. "Have mercy...."

"Oh, Fletcher. I love it when you beg."

"Kiss me. Now." He lifted his head off the pillow, straining for that soft mouth.

She gave him those warm, full lips, and he kissed her, urging her to open, which she did without even token resistance. He wrapped his arms around her and rolled, wild for her by then, wanting only the hot, perfect feel of her body closing around him.

He sought her, found her. She was slick and swollen with arousal, already wet for him. She could take him. Now. When he needed her so desperately.

He nudged her smooth thighs apart and slid inside with a pleasured moan.

Oh, the way she fit him. No one. Ever. Had fit him like that.

She wrapped those fine legs around him and she moved with him, rocking, taking his rhythms and giving them back to him, answering the questions he hadn't even known to ask.

She whispered his name, husky and low. "Fletcher..."

"Yeah," he said. "Cleo..."

And then he was rising, going up and over, spilling into her, and she was holding him, meeting him, crying out with her own release.

There was that frozen, straining moment as the pure pleasure took them. Then they both went limp.

He lifted up to his elbows and looked down into her flushed face. Her satiny throat was dewed with sweat. He bent his head and licked her there, tasting her.

"Fletcher," she whispered, breathless—and insistent. He lifted his head enough to meet her eyes. She looked…what? Disbelieving? Shocked?

He stared down at her, baffled. What the hell could be wrong? "What's the matter?"

"We forgot the condom," she said.

Chapter Eleven

Cleo thought he looked totally stunned—as stunned as *she* felt. "I can't believe we did that," she whispered.

"Damn." He blinked. Shook his head. "Neither can I."

"We've got to be more careful…." She waited for him to agree.

And he did. Kind of. "Yeah," he said. "Maybe…"

She pushed at his shoulders. "Fletcher, what do you mean *maybe?* There's no maybe about it. We have to—"

He put a finger against her lips. "Easy."

She pushed his hand away. "Fletcher, this is serious."

"We could look at this from another angle, you know"

"Another *angle?* I don't think so. We messed up. We can't afford to—"

"Wait."

"But I don't—"

"Go with me here, just for a minute."

She stared up at him, bewildered. He really was acting strangely. "Go with you…where?"

"You did tell me you wanted kids, didn't you?"

"Well, yeah. But—"

"Having sex without a condom is a good way to make that happen."

She gaped up at him. "Excuse me?"

"You heard what I said."

"Yeah. I heard it. I can't believe you said it, but I definitely heard it."

"Are you telling me you've changed your mind—that you don't want a baby, after all?"

"No. No, that's not what I said—or at least, not what I meant. What I meant was, I don't want a baby like this."

"Like what?"

She couldn't believe the look on his face. Did he find this *amusing?* She accused, "I swear, all of a sudden you are *grinning* at me."

"Yeah. So?"

"It's not funny. I don't want to be like my mother— or even like *your* mother, though that is no judgment on either of them, it's truly not. I want my kids to grow up with their father in the house, you know? I want—"

"Okay."

"Okay?" She glared up at him and demanded, *"Okay?"*

"Yeah. Okay."

She pushed at him again, hard enough that he rolled off her. Then she sat up and grabbed for the sheet at the bottom of the bed, yanking it up to cover herself. "Listen. Listen very carefully. I don't want to be a single mom. I don't want that for myself or for my kids."

"Fine. Let's get married."

Her mouth dropped open. "Would you, um, say that again?"

He put up a hand. "Wait."

"But—"

"No. I mean it. Wait right there." He slid from the bed, went to his knees, yanked open the bedside drawer and took something out of there.

"Fletcher, have you completely lost your mind?"

He shoved the drawer shut. "I think I might have." He put his fist to his chest and loudly cleared his throat. "Cleopatra. Marry me."

She clutched the sheet harder and stared down at him—naked on his knees. Proposing to her. "I…what?"

"I said, marry me." He held out his fist and opened his fingers. A gold-embossed red jewelry box sat on his spread palm. A ring box.

Her stunned gaze tracked from the box to his face and back to the box. She blinked, thinking this truly could not be real. But when she opened her eyes again, he was still on his knees, still holding out that little box. "You're serious…aren't you?"

He grinned all the wider. "Now we're getting somewhere. Give me your hand." Numbly she did. He set the little red box in it. Then he wrapped her fingers around it. "Marry me, Cleo."

A marriage proposal. From Fletcher. It was the last thing she'd ever expected to get from him. "But…why?"

He rose and sat on the bed beside her. "Well, first of all, because you're the perfect wife for me."

She swallowed. "I am?"

"You are. I knew it from that first day, when you came to my office to tell me you wouldn't, under any circumstances, put KinderWay in my casino. Cleo, you're wonderful with Ashlyn—as I knew you would be. You'll make a great mother. That's of major importance. And then there's the fact that you know and understand the world I live in—after all, you grew up in my world.

"And then there's your honesty. I look in those amber eyes and I know you'll never lie to me. I can trust you. And every time I'm near you, all I can think about is getting you naked." He tugged on the sheet she still clutched to her breasts. She didn't let go. She still couldn't quite believe this was happening. "Come on," he urged. "Say yes."

Marriage.

Fletcher wanted to marry her.

A gleeful voice inside her head was loudly shouting, *Yes!*

But she didn't say the word out loud. Not yet. She was a practical woman at heart. She might make a bold leap, but she'd get a few questions answered first.

"Fletcher?"

"Anything."

"I could never marry a man who wasn't one hundred percent true to me. If I married you, I'd have to be the only woman in your bed. Ever."

He frowned. "Haven't we already had this conversation?"

"That was about being lovers, a promise for as long as it lasted between us. This is for much, much more. This is…forever. Because that's how long I would want our marriage to last. It would be you and me, *just* you and me. Can you promise me that?"

By then, he was scowling. "I'm no virgin. I've had my share of lovers. But I would never betray my wife."

She set the red box beside her on the bed and she reached out to smooth the scowl from his brow. "Please. I'm sorry if I've offended you. But I had to know…."

He caught her hand and kissed it. "I'll be a faithful husband. Say yes."

"I, um, one more thing."

"What now?"

"Well, you've yet to mention love…."

"Love," he repeated, looking a little bit stunned.

"Yes," she said, meeting his eyes, refusing to waver. "Love."

He dropped her hand—but only long enough to pick up the red box and remove the biggest, brightest princess-cut diamond she'd ever seen. He took her left hand. It happened to be the hand she was using to hold up the sheet, which dropped around her waist. Neither of them noticed.

She was starting to put it together. "You *planned* this, didn't you?"

His expression grew severe. "The ring and the proposal, absolutely. Forgetting to use a condom—no. *That* was a mistake. The truth is, I got carried away."

"Oh, Fletcher." Her heart was pounding so hard the sound rang in her ears.

"Are you listening?"

"Oh, yes. I am."

"All right then. I love you, Cleo. Passionately. Completely. To distraction and beyond…" He slid the platinum band on her finger.

And she grabbed for him. "Oh, Fletcher. I love you, too—and yes. Yes, yes, yes!"

He caught her, turned her so she lay across his naked lap and gazed down at her, his pale eyes alight. "I think a kiss would be a good idea about now."

"I think you're right." She wrapped her arms around his neck and pulled his mouth down to hers.

Chapter Twelve

Matthew Flint turned from the window that looked out on the Strip and the Stratosphere tower looming proudly in the distance. "You've told me more than once that you would never marry a man in the gaming business."

Cleo glanced down at the diamond on her hand—the diamond she'd been wearing for just over forty-eight hours now—and then quickly back up at her father. "What can I say? I fell in love."

Flint didn't reply. He only looked at her, a long, probing sort of look. Then he strode to the wet bar against the far wall and poured himself a whisky. He glanced up before putting the stopper back in the crystal decanter. "Drink?"

"Thank you, no."

Her father picked up his glass. "What about the mechanic? You seemed so sure he was the one."

"I was. But then I met Fletcher and…that was it. I couldn't think of anyone but him. Believe me, I tried."

Flint nodded. "You've never been one to make rash decisions. I have no doubt you've given this a lot of thought."

And she had—at least, when it came to becoming Fletcher's lover. In terms of marrying him, well, maybe she hadn't been terribly thoughtful about that. For the first time in her life Cleo was wildly, madly in love. When you were madly in love and your guy proposed, there was only one answer.

Wary as she always was around the man who had fathered her, Cleo watched as Flint approached. At sixty-five he remained straight-backed and broad-shouldered. A handsome man, grown statesmanlike with age. He gestured with his whisky glass. The amber liquid swirled. "It's a beautiful ring. I'd say ten carats at least."

"Yes," she said, ill at ease with him so close. He'd been good to her, in his way. But she'd never felt as if she really knew him or even as if she might someday *come* to know him.

He raised his glass. "Bright lights, late nights." She gave him a nod and he took a sip. Not a very big one. He liked whisky, but in moderation. Power was and always had been his drug of choice. "Well." He crossed around behind his desk and dropped into his high-backed oxblood leather swivel chair. "Fletcher Bravo. I suppose I can get used to your marrying the competition. He's got talent, that Fletcher. But then, all the Bravos do. And now he and Aaron have hooked up with Jonas Bravo and his billions…sky's the limit."

She agreed. "The Bravos have done well in town."

"At least I know he can take care of you."

She couldn't let that remark pass. "I can take care of myself."

Her father chuckled. "Right you are, Cleopatra. Yes, you can."

She reached for her bag and stood. "I just wanted you to hear it from me."

He dipped his silver head in a nod. "And I thank you for that." She turned for the door. He spoke to her back. "Am I invited?"

She whirled his way again, not understanding. "To?"

His smile was wry—but his eyes weren't. "I'm assuming there will be a wedding—given that you're getting married."

She felt the heat as a blush swept up her cheeks. "Well, yes. It's this Saturday. I just never thought…" She hesitated, seeking a tactful way to say that she'd never for a moment considered that he might want to be there.

After over a decade, it still wasn't public knowledge that *the* Matthew Flint had an illegitimate daughter. He'd kept the information out of the tabloids by steering clear of situations where his name might be linked with hers. Cleo's wedding to someone as high-profile as Fletcher should have been exactly the kind of event he would want to avoid.

He said, "Inga and I are going our separate ways."

"Oh. I see." And she did.

Flint had married the world-famous supermodel, Inga Gayle, thirty-five years before. They'd had two sons together. Cleo had met Inga once, a few months after Lolita died. The still-gorgeous blonde had dropped in uninvited at Cleo's apartment. It had not been a pleasant meeting. Flint's wife had made it very clear that she didn't want her husband's bastard daughter "messing up" their lives.

Of course, your mother's trashy behavior isn't your fault, Inga had said. *But don't expect us to welcome you into our family with open arms. We'd like to keep this issue low-key. The last thing any of us wants is the sordid details spread all over the tabloids. Do I make myself clear?*

Cleo had resisted the urge to call the woman a series of very ugly names. She refused to make any deals, but she did realize that Inga *had* been betrayed and had a right to be angry. Tight-lipped, Cleo had shown her father's wife the door.

And however much she disliked Inga, Cleo hated to see a marriage—any marriage—break up. She fumbled for the right words. All she could come up with was the usual lame, "I'm so sorry."

"Don't be. We've been leading separate lives for years. The boys are adults now, self-sufficient and on their own. It's begun to seem pointless to carry on the charade. The truth is, I'm not an easy man to put up with. I guess you could say Inga has grown beyond me."

Now what was she supposed to say to that? She had a feeling he probably *was* hard to live with. He certainly hadn't been faithful. She herself was living proof of that.

He spoke into the silence between them. "Cleo, I know I haven't been any kind of real father to you. But I'd be honored if you'd allow me to attend your wedding."

Again, what could she say but, "Of course. I'm, um, pleased you want to come."

"Where and when?"

"We're keeping it simple. The wedding chapel at Impresario. Saturday at six. Family only."

"I'll be there."

And Matthew Flint *was* there. As were Fletcher's half brothers and their wives and Davey and little J.J.. Caitlin Bravo—Aaron, Will and Cade's bold and brassy mother—also attended, as did Jonas Bravo and his wife, Emma, with their toddler, Russ, and six-year-old Mandy, Jonas's adopted sister and ward. Fletcher's mother and stepdad made it, too.

And then there was Ashlyn, who, all in pink, her shining brown hair twined with rosebuds, was the cutest little flower girl Cleo had ever seen.

After the brief ceremony, they all headed over to Club Rouge, where a private room was waiting, complete with a large round table set for the wedding feast with gleaming crystal and fine china. Just about every guest had a toast to propose.

For Cleo, the evening went by in a happy blur—

except for a few moments in the ladies' lounge, where she happened to run into Caitlin.

When Cleo entered the lounge, Caitlin Bravo sat at the gold-rimmed vanity mirrors, reapplying her red-red lipstick. At the sight of Cleo, she rolled the lipstick down and capped it. "There she is, the gorgeous blushing bride!"

Cleo gave the woman a friendly smile. According to Celia, Caitlin was a wonderful person at heart. Aaron's mother had not only raised three boys on her own, she'd also made a success running a combination bar/restaurant/gift store/gaming parlor, called the Highgrade, in her hometown. "My mother-in-law didn't get where she is by keeping her mouth shut and minding her own business," Celia had warned. "If you don't want Caitlin's opinion, stay away from her. Far, far away."

Too late for that. Caitlin was already patting the red-and-gold-brocade chair next to her. "Park that pretty butt right here. Just for a moment, now, darlin'. We'll have us a quick talk, woman-to-woman."

Feeling trapped—and also a little bit curious as to what the opinionated Caitlin might have to say to her—Cleo slid into the offered seat.

Though the lounge was empty except for the two of them, Aaron's mother leaned close to Cleo, bringing with her a cloud of musky perfume. She spoke low, as if guarding against any other listening ears. "I been watching that husband of yours ever since he came to Vegas and joined up with my Aaron and his uncle Jonas. Fletcher's got those strange light eyes, now doesn't he?

Just like his daddy, that low-down SOB ex of mine. At first I thought that just lookin' in those eyes again was getting to me, that it wasn't anything about Fletcher himself that bothered me, that he only reminded me of my own checkered past and the evil, sexy man who ran me in circles—and also gave me three fine, wild sons. I have since changed my mind. It's more than just those pale eyes. It's Fletcher himself."

Alarmed, Cleo jerked back. "Why? What did he do?"

Caitlin loosed a lusty chuckle. In the bright mirror lights her hard black hair gleamed like a raven's wing. "Honey, it's nothin' he's *done,* exactly—or if it is, it's nothin' I caught him at. But there is something...."

"What?"

"Well, I don't know, not for sure. But I'll lay odds something is bothering him in a deep way. There's some secret he's keeping. With him, no one gets too close."

"You know this...how?"

"I know it *here.*" Caitlin fisted a hand and pounded her chest with it. "And I also know that you're the woman to open him up."

"Er...you do?" Cleo's apprehension faded as she realized that Caitlin was quite a character—but not necessarily anyone Cleo needed to take too seriously.

Caitlin loosed a hefty sigh, and the bright beads on her red dress glittered madly with the movement. "I didn't get me three sons by a psychopath without learnin' a thing or two about what goes on in men's minds. I been worried about Fletcher, I truly have.

Worried not knowing how he'd ever allow himself to let down his guard and find the love every man needs. But tonight I met you, sweetheart. And I can honestly say I'm not worried anymore. You're the woman that he has been waiting for."

Cleo resisted the urge to make some flippant remark concerning Caitlin's amazing psychic abilities. No. That would be cruel. Caitlin meant well. Cleo could see her sincerity in her black eyes. "Well. I, um, promise to do my best."

Caitlin laughed her raucous laugh again. "You don't believe a thing I've told you, now do you? And don't answer that. I've said what needed sayin' and that's all she wrote for this particular conversation." She grabbed her sequined bag and pushed herself to her feet. "I wish you health, wealth and love aplenty, darlin', on this your wedding day." Then she turned for the door and went out without looking back, her high red heels tapping hard on the black marble floor.

The next morning Cleo and Fletcher took off for a Bravo-owned five-star resort in Cabo San Lucas. Fletcher's mother and stepdad stayed with Ashlyn at the penthouse for the four brief days they were gone.

Those four days were beautiful. Cleo and her new husband lay in the tropical sun and swam in the blue, blue sea and made love—a lot.

Twice—the afternoon of the first day of their honeymoon and two days later at dinner—Cleo found herself thinking that her groom seemed just a little preoccupied, a little bit withdrawn. Both times she asked him if something was bothering him. Both times he reassured her that there was absolutely nothing wrong.

The second time she asked, at dinner on their private balcony overlooking the beach and the fabulous jewel-blue ocean, he reached across the table. She gave him her hand and reveled, as always, in the sheer thrill of his touch.

"How could I be preoccupied?" he said. "I'm right where I want to be—with you."

They returned home midweek, said goodbye to Fletcher's folks and then they both rushed around playing catch-up, getting on top of what hadn't gotten done while they'd been lying in the sun. Fletcher had a series of killer meetings that stretched into the evening on both Thursday and Friday, so Cleo and Ashlyn shared dinner on their own.

Friday night, Cleo was sound asleep long before Fletcher returned to the penthouse. Deep in the hours between midnight and dawn, she stirred, opened her eyes—and stared into the darkness at Fletcher's side of the bed.

Empty.

She stretched out a hand, felt the cool, undisturbed expanse of silk. The red numerals on his bedside clock read 3:13. So very late. Where could he be? He'd said nothing about being gone all night.

Restless and beginning to worry, she rolled over.

And there he was, sitting in the buff leather easy chair five feet from the bed. His bow tie was undone and his collar unbuttoned, but otherwise he was fully dressed in a gorgeous black tux.

She canted up on an elbow and pushed her tangled hair out of her eyes. "Hey. There you are. I was just wondering what might have happened to you…."

"Late night," he said, his voice a low, soft rumble, his gaze never straying, trained on her. "Entertaining the whales."

"Gotta keep those high rollers happy."

"That's right. How's Ashlyn been?"

"Very proud. She finished *The Happy Ladybug* tonight."

"How did it end?"

"Happily." She sent him a grin.

He didn't grin back. "For some reason, I'm not surprised." His gaze, shining and somber, didn't leave her face. "I did stop by her room to check on her."

"And?"

"Out like a light." He continued to watch her as he began to undress.

Swiftly, almost brutally, he yanked off his tie, shrugged out of his jacket, unbuttoned his shirt. He dropped the fine clothes to the floor by the chair as he shed them.

Bare-chested, he shucked off his black Italian dress shoes and slipped off his socks, the muscles of his lean arms and strong shoulders bunching and flexing with each deft, deliberate move he made. Once the shoes and socks were off, he stood. Down went the black tux slacks and his silk boxers, too.

Naked—and fully aroused—he came for her. She lifted the covers, a thrilling sense of mingled alarm and excitement skittering through her. He slid in beside her and gathered her to him, rolling so that he was on top, then easing himself between her thighs, his lean body pressing her down. Below, he nudged at her, a delirious, insistent pressure. He smelled faintly of brandy and expensive cigars, reminding her of where he had been—out wining and dining Impresario's biggest-spending guests.

She looked up into those gleaming eyes and wasn't sure what she saw there. "Fletcher? Are you…angry?"

"No," he whispered. "Not at all."

And then he kissed her.

Oh, she couldn't think when he was kissing her. She twined her arms around his neck and kissed him back as he pushed on her short satin nightgown, easing it up over her belly, his hands molding her flesh in the hungriest, most thrilling way.

He lifted his body away from hers—just a little, enough that his fingers could find her. His intimate touch sent her soaring even higher. She wanted him desperately, wanted…

All of him. Now.

She reached down between them, clasped his heat and hardness—and guided him home.

They both moaned at the glorious pleasure of entry. And then he lifted up on his elbows and looked down at her, eyes burning even brighter than before, as he moved in her—moved *with* her.

She gazed up at him, her body dissolving, going molten, and she wondered how she could love him so much—love him and sometimes be absolutely certain that she didn't know him at all, her lover, her husband, the man who was everything she'd sworn *never* to love.

And yet, by some dark and wondrous miracle, she did love him. Madly. Wildly. Without reservation. In a reckless way her cautious heart had never thought to know.

She whispered, "I love you, Fletcher. I love you so...."

He muttered, "Cleo." The word was rough in his throat, full of heat and yearning—and something that sounded almost like pain.

They both went still, straining at the peak, pushing into each other as if they might somehow make their separate bodies one. And then came that wonderful, loosening rush of pure feeling, and she was going over, riding a giant glittering waterfall of sensation down into a velvety midnight scattered with bright-burning stars.

The next morning, Saturday, he was already gone from the bed when she woke. She pushed back the covers and went to look for him in the bathroom.

He wasn't there either, but she recognized that faint humid scent of soap and aftershave. He'd already showered and gone. Quickly she showered, too.

As she pulled on a sweater and jeans, she found herself wondering again if something might be bothering him. They'd been married a week and somehow every day he seemed just a little bit farther away from her.

Out of nowhere, Andrea Raye's spiteful words drifted into her mind.

Some men just aren't the forever type. They like to go after you, they like to love you up... But once you're caught, it can get old really fast for them....

She also remembered what Caitlin had said in the ladies' lounge on Cleo's wedding day.

But I'll lay odds something is bothering him in a deep way. There's some secret he's keeping. With him, no one gets too close....

Cleo turned to the mirror on the dressing room wall and scowled at her own reflection. Not smart, to let some thoroughly out-of-line remark of Andrea's get to her or to take seriously the wild ideas of the eccentric Caitlin. The dancer had admitted that she was jealous, that she still carried a torch for Fletcher. And Caitlin, well, what she'd said about Fletcher was only her opinion, no matter how vehemently she'd insisted it was true.

No. If something was bothering Fletcher, he would confide in Cleo eventually. He loved her. He *trusted* her. He had said so himself the night he proposed.

And since then, whispered a sly voice in her head, *he hasn't said he loves you again.*

He hadn't. Not once. Except for during their wedding

vows, obliquely, when he'd promised—as all grooms do—to love, honor and cherish his bride.

"Shut up," she said aloud to silence her own negative thoughts.

Sheesh. What was the matter with her? Had marrying the man she loved turned her into a whiny clinging vine? Was she suddenly someone who needed constant reassurance that her man adored her and would never stray?

Uh-uh. She was a self-sufficient person with a job she loved and a fulfilling life—even before you added her gorgeous, sexy husband and adorable stepdaughter to the mix. Whining and clinging simply weren't her style.

She brushed her hair and put a big smile on her face and went out to the kitchen, where she found Fletcher and Ashlyn already at the breakfast table.

"There you are, you sleepyhead Cleo." Ashlyn held out her arms. Cleo went over and gave her a quick hug. She sent Fletcher a bright smile. "Mornin'."

"Good morning." He didn't smile back—but his eyes said he remembered the heat and wonder of a few hours before. Cleo took a seat and Mrs. Dolby served her the usual poached eggs on toast.

That day, since Fletcher had to work, Cleo took Ashlyn to her house in Summerlin.

"We are packing things up today," Cleo explained once she'd led the little girl inside.

"Packing things up," Ashlyn repeated with great seriousness. Then she frowned. "Why?"

"Because I live with you and your daddy now."

"And I like that!"

"Me, too. But it means I don't need this little house anymore. So I'm going to put a lot of my things in boxes and tape them up and sell some and give some away—and store the rest. And then I'll put the house on the market."

Ashlyn was frowning again. "Cleo, even if it's not a big house, I think it will still be much, much too heavy."

Cleo constantly marveled at the literal nature of the five-year-old mind. "You mean, too heavy to lift and put *on the market?*"

"Yes." Ashlyn nodded, very solemn.

So Cleo explained what the phrase *on the market* meant, after which the two of them got to work.

They started in the kitchen. Cleo assigned Ashlyn the job of boxing up the drawers of utensils and the pots and pans in the lower cabinets—all easy-to-reach sturdy stuff that wasn't likely to suffer at the mercy of eager five-year-old hands.

There was much clanging of pots and clinking of flatware, but within an hour Ashlyn had packed four boxes in her own enthusiastic but not in the least organized style. About then she started losing interest. So Cleo led her to the living room and turned on the Disney channel. Ashlyn perched among the sofa pillows and Cleo returned to packing up the kitchen.

At the back of a high cupboard she found a blue mug with *Danny* printed on it in bold red letters. He'd brought it over last fall and teased her that it was his own personal mug and she'd better never use it....

The memory kind of tugged at her heartstrings. He was such a great guy. She'd forgotten the mug that final evening when she'd been gathering up his things for him. Not a big deal. She would mail it to him.

When she started in on her bedroom, she found an old T-shirt of his with *Head Mechanic* on the front of it in gothic script. She also found a pair of flip-flops he'd left and a studded black leather belt. It made her feel sentimental to see those things of Danny's, to gather them up and put them in a box to send to him.

He'd been a good friend. She hated to lose him, but sometimes you had to make choices in life. You couldn't have everything, that was just the way it was. She knew that she'd hurt Danny. And also that the best thing she could do for him—and for herself—was let him go and move on.

She worked until noon, then she and Ashlyn returned to the penthouse at Impresario. They'd left Fletcher at work in his study. He was gone when they returned.

Mrs. Dolby had a message from him. "He said to tell you he had a few things to take care of that just couldn't wait."

Ashlyn shook her head. "My daddy is so busy."

"He certainly is," Cleo agreed. She put on a bright smile for her stepdaughter. "Well. Shall we make ourselves some sandwiches?"

"Okay," said Ashlyn. "And then, after lunch, I think I'll write another book."

* * *

Again that night Fletcher didn't come home until late. Cleo woke when he pulled back the covers. He reached for her. She wrapped her arms around him, breathed in the masculine scent of him....

And realized as she did it that she was checking for the scent of another woman.

But no. There was nothing. Just Fletcher and his heat and his wonderful kisses. She looked in his eyes while he was loving her and all her nagging doubts flew away.

He was her husband. She loved him and he loved her and everything would be okay.

A little later, after the loving, as they lay side by side and she was just drifting toward sleep, he turned his head her way. "There's a box addressed to your old boyfriend on the table in the foyer...."

She tried to read his eyes through the shadows: jealous? Suspicious? Merely curious? She couldn't have said. "I found some things of his while I was packing up over at my house. I'll mail them back to him tomorrow."

"You miss him?"

She told the truth, though she knew a lie would have been easier. "A little. He's...a good person. He was a good friend."

"Yeah." Somehow he made the word just a little bit threatening. "He seemed like a real nice guy."

"He is—and Fletcher?"

"Yeah."

"I haven't seen him since he broke it off with me. And I won't see him. I think it's, um, better that way."

He reached across and clasped her shoulder, pulling her toward him, guiding her onto her side. He shifted, too—and they were facing each other. "I not only *think* it's better," he whispered, "I *know* it is."

She gave him a quivery smile and pressed her body to his, reveling as she always did in the very feel of him. At the cove where her thighs met, he stirred and hardened. She felt her own body melting, yearning, readying for him all over again.

He dipped his dark head and captured her mouth. She gave her kiss willingly, opening to the wet thrust of his seeking tongue. His lean, knowing hands cupped her breasts….

Oh, this truly was heaven, making love with this man. This was when she really *knew* him, when she never felt cut off or distant from him, never wondered if he kept secrets he would never share.

Those magic hands of his went wandering, stroking, arousing. His mouth left hers to kiss her neck, the hollow of her throat, the wings of her collarbones.

He pushed back the covers, called her beautiful and kissed her all over, finally lifting her thighs and settling them over his shoulders to give her the most intimate kisses of all. His tongue claimed her, stroking her, *knowing* her.

She shattered in seconds with a sharp cry. Then he

swept up her body and she knew he meant to bury himself deep in her eager wetness.

But she didn't let him. Oh, no. She pushed on his chest until he gave in and lay back.

And then she exacted her erotic revenge. She kissed him as he'd kissed her—all over, with great care. Then she took him, so hard and ready, in her hand and she lowered her mouth slowly down over him. He let out a low cry then, and she smiled as she lifted her mouth— and lowered it down over him once more.

Groaning, he caught her head between his strong hands, fingers splayed in her hair. She lowered her mouth again—and again he cried out.

"Can't wait." He groaned. "Now, Cleo. Here, with me. Now…"

So she moved up his body, claiming his lips, and slowly, by agonizing degrees, she lowered herself onto him.

They didn't last long. Behind her eyelids she saw stars. And then he was grabbing her, rolling her beneath him.

They sailed over the edge together, flying, soaring— and coming to rest at last in their own bed, held close in each other's arms.

Close.

Yes. She did feel close to him then, in those glorious moments when they found ecstasy together. But the rest of the time?

No.

The next day it was the same. He worked late and got home after she was asleep. Tuesday, the same thing again. And Wednesday, as well.

His absence was becoming routine. There was never time to talk, never an opportunity to discuss what seemed to be happening between them—the distance that yawned greater each day.

At night, late, when he finally came to bed, he would take her in his arms and love her, and for those too-brief shining moments, held close in his arms, she would be certain that this was just a phase they were going through, that his workload was extra heavy right now. That soon things would settle down and they'd get a little quality time together.

Somehow, though, it never happened. Two weeks went by during which she knew him mostly in the dark, as the passionate lover who woke her from sleep to work his seductive magic on her willing flesh.

When she did see him during daylight hours, it was usually at the breakfast table, with Ashlyn. And that wasn't the right time to bring up the way they seemed to be drifting apart—or rather, the way they'd never quite found each other in the first place.

Cleo ran her business. She packed up her house in Summerlin and got it listed with a Realtor. And she took care of her stepdaughter.

Ashlyn…

That relationship, at least, was going well—better than well.

Cleo felt that she and her stepdaughter were forming a true and unbreakable bond. Fletcher's little girl was the child of her heart. Cleo stopped thinking of Ashlyn as Fletcher's. She easily slipped into the lovely habit of treating Ashlyn as her own.

On a Saturday evening near the end of March, three weeks after the wedding, Cleo and her stepdaughter were playing Old Maid on the floor in the family room.

Ashlyn glanced up from her cards. "Cleo?"

Cleo studied her hand, rearranging the cards. "Hmm?"

"I think you'd better just be my mommy, okay?"

Cleo's throat clutched at those words. She set her cards aside and put all of her attention on Ashlyn. She looked into those dark eyes, scanned that wonderful oh-so-serious little face. "Honey, I am your mom. Your stepmom."

"Well, but I just want to call you Mommy. Will that be okay?"

What a moment. The kind a mother cherishes forever. "I would love it if you called me Mommy."

Ashlyn smiled, a slow smile, a smile made all the more precious by its rarity. She tossed down her cards and threw herself into Cleo's open arms. Those small, soft hands went around her neck and held on tight.

"Big hug," said Ashlyn squeezing hard. Then she craned back in Cleo's embrace. "Mommy," she said firmly, with feeling, and smiled again. Cleo grabbed her close once more, rocking back and forth, holding on tight. And then Ashlyn whispered, "Don't you ever, ever go away."

"I won't," Cleo promised. "Not ever."

As she made the vow, she found herself thinking of Fletcher, of their marriage that didn't feel much like a marriage at all. Where had it gone wrong?

Or rather, why wouldn't he give it a chance to be right?

She loved him. She truly did. And she loved his daughter as her own.

But he was hardly ever with them. It wasn't right. One way or another, this absentee-husband thing just had to stop.

Chapter Thirteen

That night, when Fletcher finally came home, Cleo was sitting in the bedside chair, fully dressed and waiting for him. With the lights out.

She watched him come in. He opened the door slowly, slipped through and closed it with care. Then he approached the bed, not exactly tiptoeing but almost.

He was halfway through the sitting area before he saw her. "Cleo." He stopped in midstep. "What are you doing up?" Through the shadows she couldn't make out his expression, but his voice was as careful as his steps had been.

She reached back and flipped on the floor lamp by her chair. "Waiting for you."

In the wash of lamplight his face gave nothing away. "In the dark?"

"I was afraid if I left the light on, you might not come in."

He frowned. "Why wouldn't I?"

She shrugged. "You tell me."

Something flashed in his eyes—and was quickly banished. He went to the bed and dropped to the edge of it. "What a night. I had to hang around in the casino. Tokuru was talking dinner at midnight. And what he wants, I try to make sure that he gets." Machu Tokuru was a Japanese businessman. A whale to end all whales. When he gambled, he'd been known to drop millions a night playing blackjack or craps.

Fletcher's tux was midnight-blue, with silk shirt and satin tie to match. He stretched his neck the way men do and fiddled with the lustrous tie until it fell loose. He took off his tux jacket, laid it on the bed. Then came the cufflinks and the shirt studs. He took off his shirt. And then, bare to the waist, he gathered up the clothes he'd taken off and disappeared into the walk-in closet.

When he came back out, he was naked. He strode toward her, all lean muscle and sleek male grace. When he reached her chair, he put out his hand. "Come on."

"Where?"

A pause. Then, low and rough, he said, "To bed."

She looked up at him, saw the heat in his eyes, the promise of lovely, dark pleasures. And she wanted to simply put her hand in his, let him undress her, share with him the beauty of the night. At least they had that—incredible sex.

But no. It wasn't right. There should be more. And there *had* been more—at first. Hadn't there?

Sometimes lately she found herself wondering if it had all been some kind of terrible mistake. They'd been lovers for less than two weeks when he proposed. Nine days. How could you really know a person in that time?

Right now she felt that she didn't know him at all and she had no idea how to *begin* to know him. How could that be? It had all seemed so easy, so effortless, at the beginning, so perfect and right.

From that Thursday they'd met in the hallway and ended up here in his bedroom as lovers—from then until the night he proposed—she'd been stunned by the wonder his mere touch could bring. She'd never given a thought to the idea of marriage. Loving Fletcher had been her ultimate guilty pleasure, something that could never last.

And then he'd proposed, said he loved her, said he *trusted* her....

Yes had seemed the only answer at the time.

But since then she'd become slowly aware that she was climbing a glass mountain, getting nowhere with him. One step upward—and then a quick slide to the bottom again. Never making any real progress.

As Andrea Raye had warned her.

As Caitlin Bravo had intuitively known.

"Fletcher..."

His outstretched hand dropped to his side. "What?" The single flatly spoken word did nothing to bolster her confidence.

She forged ahead anyway. "It seems like since we got married I hardly see you. Is there...something wrong?"

He stood very still before her, his lean-muscled body gloriously naked, his heart and mind a complete mystery to her. "Nothing's wrong. I know I've been busy. But you know how my work is." He sounded so logical, so perfectly reasonable. And so very far away. "Sometimes there just aren't enough hours in the day...."

"It's not only that."

"Oh?" He looked...tired. As if he only wished she'd give it up and let him lead her to bed.

Again she considered doing just that, letting the tough subject go, rising, taking off her clothes, turning off the light.

But no. She did want more from her marriage than a man who could love her with his body alone. She wanted his heart. She wanted to give him all her secrets and for him to share his with her.

She said, "It's more than just that we hardly see each other."

"What else?" The words were guarded.

"Look, I know your job is demanding. I can accept that. My job is, too. Still, there ought to be a little time every day just for the two of us. Time when we're really together. But I don't feel...together with you. I haven't since we got married. You seem to avoid me, avoid any situation where we might be alone, just the two of us, unless it's the middle of the night and we're making love. It's as if you don't want to talk to me, as if you're afraid to get caught alone with me if there's a chance we might end up saying things that matter, as if you're…hiding something and you're afraid I might find out."

Did he blink? Had she hit a nerve, gotten close to whatever it was that kept them apart? She couldn't be sure. The strange, frantic look in his eyes was already gone—if it had ever really been there at all.

"You're saying you want more time with me?"

Well, duh. "Yes." She felt a smile quiver across her mouth and then fade. It wasn't only the time. "Oh, Fletcher. It's…the closeness. The talking, the sharing…"

"All right," he said flatly.

She wanted to leap up, grab those big shoulders, give him a hard shake. But she only swallowed and gently asked, "All right…what?"

"Whatever you want. Just tell me. It's yours." He extended his hand again. "Now come to bed."

With a long sigh she laid her hand in his. Though she knew she hadn't gotten through to him in the way she'd hoped she might, she wanted his lean arms around her. She needed the reassurance of physical contact right then. He pulled her up against his broad, warm chest.

She rested her hands on his powerful shoulders and she looked up into those incredible eyes. "Oh, Fletcher. I love you."

He brought his mouth down on hers. His kiss was

deep and hot and so exciting. It could almost banish her doubts and her fears. As he kissed her, he undressed her, peeling her clothes off, dropping them to the floor.

"Tomorrow," she whispered, as he guided her down to their bed. "It's Easter. Stay home with us."

"I will," he promised. "I will."

And he did. He stayed with them for all of the following day. In the morning, they went over to Celia's and the adults hid Easter eggs right there in the big apartment. The kids hunted them down. They stayed for lunch and went back to their own place around two. When dinnertime came, they sent out for Chinese.

Monday and Tuesday, Cleo hardly saw Fletcher, but Wednesday night, he had a dinner appointment with a couple of bigwigs. He took Cleo along. It wasn't the most fun she'd ever had, being charming for strangers, playing the CEO's wife. Still, she was at her husband's side; they were spending the time together that she had so craved.

As one day faded into the next, he did make an effort. He stayed home a little more and he made himself available for family time and for just the two of them.

But Cleo still had the strangest, most troubling feeling that he was holding something back from her—that he kept his heart closed.

And he'd yet to say again that he loved her. That did bother her.

Should she just ask him? Over and over, she rehearsed how she might say it.

Fletcher, you've only said you love me once, on the day you proposed. I can't help wondering…do you? Love me, I mean?

Ick.

She knew she would only sound pitiful and needy. Really, shouldn't a man have the sense to tell his wife he loved her, to let her know every once in a while that she was the woman who held his heart?

If she *was* the woman who held his heart…

Far back in her mind, Andrea's words still taunted.

Some men just aren't the forever type… Once you're caught, it can get old really fast….

Oh, this whole thing was just so damn confusing. She needed…a sounding board, a little good advice.

She trusted Celia absolutely. She could talk to her. But she wondered about the wisdom of revealing her marital issues to Fletcher's sister-in-law. That didn't seem right, to put Celia in the middle between her brother-in-law and his wife. So she kept her mouth shut.

But then, on the first Friday in April, Jane and Jilly came back to town for a visit and Celia invited Cleo to her penthouse for lunch.

"More wine?" Celia had brought the bottle into the living room after they'd left the table.

Cleo put her hand over her glass. "Better not. Remember last time."

Jilly chuckled and held up her glass for a refill. "Well, I don't know." Celia filled the glass. "Last time worked out pretty well, as I remember. You got your worries off your chest. And then you ran into the man of your dreams in the hallway…and the rest, as they say, is history. All because of that second glass of wine."

"Hmm," said Cleo. "I never thought of it that way…." Celia held up the bottle again. Cleo laughed. "Uh-uh. I mean it. I really will pass."

Celia grinned and set it on the coffee table. "It's right here if you change your mind."

"Good to know."

Jane adjusted her maternity jumper over her burgeoning belly and reached for her glass of cranberry juice. "The main thing is that you're in the family now. We're all happy about that. Ashlyn deserves a wonderful mother like you. And I've always said that what Fletcher needs is the right wife."

Cleo sat forward and asked with a lot more urgency than she intended, "You really think I'm the right wife for him?"

"Yes." Jane replied with a firm nod. "I'm absolutely certain you're the right woman for him."

"Sometimes, I have to admit, I wonder…."

Jilly set down her wineglass. "Okay. What's going on? Is something wrong?"

Cleo looked from Jilly to Jane to Celia and back to Jilly again. "Oh, I wasn't going to do this. I truly was not…."

"Sure you were," said Celia. "And it's *good* that you were. Sometimes you just need to talk to a friend—or three, if they all happen to be available."

"It's only…" Cleo's voice wandered off into nothing again.

Jane said, "Come on. It's okay."

"You know you want to tell us," said Jilly.

"That's right," said Celia. "And we only want to help."

Cleo believed them. And she really did need to talk about it. "Well, sometimes I feel I don't even know him."

"Not good," murmured Jane.

"That's a problem," agreed Jilly.

Cleo elaborated. "We got married so fast. Maybe too fast. We should have taken it more slowly, should have gotten to know each other better…but we didn't. And now, well, I feel as if I don't have the faintest idea what's in his heart. He doesn't *talk* to me, not really. He's not…open to me." She shook her head, raked her fingers back through her hair. "Oh, God. I don't know. Am I making any sense at all?"

"You are," said Celia.

"We understand." Jane was nodding. Jilly was, too.

Cleo admitted, "Sometimes I wonder if this is my problem and not his. I mean, it's not as if I grew up in a happy nuclear family, not as if I have a lot of experience with what makes a good marriage work. My mom raised me on her own. With her, there was always a new man, he was always the love of her life—until it was over and she went out looking for the next one. Maybe I just don't get the way it is between a man and a woman when they're married. But then I think of Danny and…"

"Hello?" Jilly was frowning. "Who's Danny?"

"He was my boyfriend when I met Fletcher. I fell for Fletcher. And Danny broke it off with me. And he was right to break it off, because, from the moment I first saw Fletcher, I knew he was the man for me—though I fought it and fought it hard. But with Danny it was kind of like with you guys, here, now. Until Fletcher came on the scene and Danny and I started growing apart, I honestly felt that Danny was *open* to me, that he let me in his heart, you know?"

"And you *don't* feel that way with Fletcher?" Celia's question was really more of a statement.

"No, I don't. I'm long-gone in love with him. I can't imagine my life without him in it. He's the only man for me and yet…" She pressed both hands against her cheeks. "Oh, how can I be so much in love with someone and still feel like I don't know him at all?" She confessed low, "And I have to tell you guys, this is pretty much what Caitlin said would happen."

"Whoa." Jilly knocked back a big slug of wine. "Caitlin. As in—" she gestured to Jane, to Celia and then to herself "—our mother-in-law?"

Cleo nodded, feeling bleak. "Caitlin said she knew that Fletcher had secrets—and that she was sure I was the woman to open him up. So far, that is definitely not happening."

Celia was looking slightly bewildered. "I don't get it. When did you talk to Caitlin about Fletcher?"

"On my wedding day, in the ladies' lounge at Club Rouge."

Celia blinked. "But…why?"

"You'd have to ask Caitlin. She was in there powdering her nose. I walked in—and she wouldn't let me go without a 'woman-to-woman' talk."

"Scar-ee," declared Jilly.

Jane asked the pertinent question. "What did Caitlin say?"

Cleo filled them in.

When she was through, Celia scoffed, "Well, trust Caitlin to make Fletcher's natural reserve into some deep, dark secret he's keeping from everyone."

"Now wait a minute." Jane supported her big belly with a cradling hand and shifted on the sofa, sitting up a little straighter. "Caitlin can drive us nuts, but she *is* perceptive. You both know that she is."

"Oh, but come on," groaned Jilly. "She's also the kind who never spoils a good story with too much hard fact."

Jane looked at Cleo. "Have you tried to talk to Fletcher? I mean, really made a serious effort, sat him down and explained to him that you feel cut off from him, that you want more time with him?"

"Yes. I have. Last Sunday night. And I think the part about spending more time together might have actually sunk in. Since we talked—or rather, since *I* talked and he stared at me like I was from some other planet—he *has* been home more, with *us* more, me and Ashlyn."

Jilly said, "Okay. I can't stop myself. I've gotta ask. The sex. Is it…?"

Cleo shrugged. "Incredible. Fabulous. The earth moves and the stars explode."

"Oh. Well, then. Not a sex problem."

"No. I'd have to say, if sex made a marriage, I'd be the happiest woman on Earth. Scratch that—in the universe. Oh, I don't know. If he would only say he loves me…"

Glances ricocheted between the other three women. Then Jane cleared her throat. "He's never said he loves you?"

"Once. The morning he proposed. And I really believed him then. That day, I had no doubt he loved me completely, that I was everything he wanted in a woman *and* in a wife. But since then…"

Jilly suggested, *"Nada?"*

"That's it. Nothing. Not a word—and you don't need to ask if I say I love *him*. I do. All the time."

"Well." Jane paused for another sip of juice. "Maybe that's your next move."

Cleo swallowed. "Uh, what?"

"Ask him if he loves you."

Jilly chuckled. "Jane's always been the one for getting it right out there—except with Cade. She was a little bit backward when it came to Cade."

"A *little* backward." Celia gave a delicate snort. "She was in total denial when it came to Cade."

"Maybe I was." Jane patted her big tummy. "But look at us now." She turned her dark glance to Cleo again. "I say, if it's bothering you, ask him. Say, *Fletcher I love you. Do you love me?* And then shut up. Resist the urge to backpedal. And don't you dare answer for him."

Jilly agreed. "Jane's right."

Celia thought so, too. "Ask the question. And let him take it from there."

That night, Fletcher was supposed to be home at eight, but the hours stretched out as they so often did. Cleo went to bed.

And eventually he joined her.

He slid in beside her and took her in his arms and kissed her. She pulled back before he could do more and asked him the big question simply and directly.

"Fletcher, I love you. Do you love me?"

His eyes gleamed through the shadows. "Yes," he whispered. "I do."

Chapter Fourteen

"So that was it," Cleo told Celia Sunday morning when their husbands were working, J.J. was napping and Ashlyn and Davey had wandered off to play in Ashlyn's room. "Asked and answered, as they say on *Law & Order*."

"Did you believe him?"

"I did."

"Well, then…"

"He loves me," Cleo said. "I'm willing to call that pretty much settled—he loves me." She said it again, wondering who she was trying to convince.

Celia wasn't fooled. "But?"

"He just won't *talk* to me. And contrary to Caitlin's

prediction that I was the woman to open him up, I'm starting to think that's never going to happen."

Celia shook her head. "I wish I had some brilliant suggestion for making things all better."

Cleo sighed. "You listen. It means a lot."

Maybe, Cleo thought as she lay in bed that night waiting for Fletcher, this really was *her* problem and not his. Maybe she wanted more from him than she had a right to ask.

He'd said he loved her. She did believe him. Shouldn't that be enough?

Was she more damaged by her fatherless childhood than she'd understood until now? She couldn't help doubting herself, wondering if the real issue here was that she hadn't a clue how to love a man in any deep, abiding way, so she blamed the man for her own inadequacies.

Fletcher worked hard. He was good to her and to his daughter. He made love to her often, with great skill and, much more important, with enthusiasm. Andrea Raye's bitter remarks to the contrary, Fletcher *wasn't* bored with his wife now that he'd caught her—at least, not in the sexual sense. Cleo believed he stayed true to her. She just couldn't see him being so sexually attentive if he had some other woman on the side.

So, truthfully, what was the matter here?

What was the problem?

Just maybe there *was* no problem. It could very well be that her doubts and dissatisfactions with her marriage were all in her head and she really needed to get the heck past them.

Across the room the door to the hallway opened. A tall, lean figure slipped through. She watched his shadow moving toward her.

When he reached the bed, she held up her arms.

"What's this?" he asked, his voice low and rough and oh-so-sexy.

"Me," she said. "Waiting for you."

It was all right, Cleo told herself over and over in the next couple of weeks. Even if sometimes she felt he was a million miles away from her, Fletcher did love her. He tried to make time to spend with her. His kisses swept her away.

And there was Ashlyn, who now called her Mommy, who smiled more often as each day went by. Cleo couldn't imagine how she'd ever gotten along without Ashlyn to light up her days as Fletcher did her nights.

But now and then it would come to her, sharp as a stabbing knife, that things really weren't as they should be with Fletcher. Sometimes it happened at night, when he would come home to her and make love to her and never say a word unless she spoke first.

And sometimes it would happen when they were all three together at the breakfast table or in the evening after dinner when they'd retire to the family room. Cleo would glance over at him and he would have the strangest, saddest, most lost look on his handsome face—as if she and Ashlyn were on the other side of a thick glass wall from him, a wall both unbreakable and much too high to scale.

She would know for certain at that moment that Caitlin had been right. Something terrible was troubling him. She would think, *Tell me, my darling. You can trust me. You* can…

And the moment would pass. The look would vanish from his face as if it had never been. She would wonder if she'd seen that lost expression at all. Maybe she'd only *wanted* to see it, wanted to believe there was some secret he could share with her that would change everything, would make her feel close to him in that special, indefinable, emotional way.

Then she missed her period.

Cleo had the kind of menstrual cycle you could set your clock by. She was due the tenth. By the eighteenth, when her period still hadn't come, she bought a home test. She took that test the next morning and got the answer she craved.

Pregnant.

Cleo floated through the day with a wide grin on her face. Both Megan, her associate director, and Kelly, her assistant at the original KinderWay, mentioned how cheerful she was that day. She smiled all the wider and told them yes, she was feeling terrific, on top of the world. She couldn't wait for Fletcher to get home so she could share her wonderful news.

A baby. They would have a baby. Another little one

for her to love. Oh, she could just see Ashlyn as a big sister, see that little blue- or pink-wrapped bundle in those five-year-old arms....

That night, after she put Ashlyn to bed, Cleo waited up in the living room until ten, longing for her husband to come through the door so she could throw herself into his arms, kiss him passionately and then whisper gleefully, *It's happened. I'm pregnant. We'll have a baby by Christmas.*

He called at ten-fifteen to say he was sorry but he'd be another hour at least. So she went to bed and lay awake, waiting some more, rehearsing the way she would tell him the news.

But as midnight went by and he still hadn't come home, her mind took a detour. She found herself thinking of Fletcher's first wife, wondering how Belinda had told him that *she* was pregnant with the baby who would turn out to be Ashlyn. Hadn't Fletcher said she'd asked for a divorce at the same time?

So very sad. They'd split up before Ashlyn was born.

It still nagged at Cleo, deep down, that he'd let Ashlyn vanish from his life like that. She really didn't understand what had gone wrong between him and Belinda to make the split so complete that he'd even turned his back on his child.

And yes, she did wonder if his problems in his first marriage had their roots in that emotional distance he maintained between himself and other people. He had told her that it was all about Belinda's dislike of the gaming industry and how she missed her hometown.

But he'd also admitted that he'd never had much time to spend with her.

Cleo didn't care a whole lot for the industry either. After the kind of childhood she'd known, she had more than a few ingrained prejudices against it; bright lights and late nights were just not her style.

And Fletcher didn't exactly lavish her with his time and undivided attention. If she had a nice hometown to go to and loving parents waiting there for her, she just might be drawn back to them. And once safe in the care of a family that cherished her, she might be reluctant to return to a world she disliked and a husband who wouldn't—or couldn't—love her the way she wanted to be loved.

In the darkness Cleo blinked hard and shook her head against the doubts she could never quite banish.

Just look at her. Going *there* again. Obsessing over that indefinable something that was lacking in her marriage. Wishing Fletcher could be someone he clearly wasn't. She sat up, switched on the bedside lamp and grabbed the book on child development that waited on the nightstand.

She'd just finished the first chapter when the door to the hallway opened—and there he was, the unknowable man she loved, dressed for the nightlife in one of his fifteen tailor-made tuxes, looking killer-handsome and just a little bit tired. She bookmarked her page and set the volume back on the nightstand.

Fletcher dropped into the easy chair next to the bed. "You didn't have to wait up."

She gave him a tight smile. "I know." Her wonderful news seemed—what? Not the issue anymore, not the thing she really wanted—*needed*—to say to him. She watched him as she had so many nights before. He loosened and removed his tie, his jacket, his cufflinks, his shirt.

He bent to untie his handmade black shoes. He was on the second set of laces when he slanted her a look— one that questioned and yet somehow managed to warn at the same time. *What's on your mind?* the look said. *But don't tell me, because I don't want to hear.*

She ignored the warning and went with the question. "What *really* went wrong between you and Belinda?"

There was a silence. A long one. Taking his sweet time about it, he removed his shoes. Once he had them both off, he lined them up like good little soldiers beside the chair. Then and only then did he sit back with a weighty sigh. "I thought we went through all that weeks ago."

"Yes. But I still don't really understand...." How to say it? How to get him, at last, to trust her, to open up to her.

"What?" He asked the question in a patient tone— too patient, really. "You don't understand what?"

Cleo tugged on the blankets, smoothing them more snugly across her breasts. "You know, maybe I *do* understand. Maybe that's the real problem for me, as your *current* wife. I do understand why Belinda left you— or at least, I can guess why. Because I think that you probably treat me the same way you treated her."

His strong jaw was set. He sat in that chair as if he'd been carved out of stone. "All right," he said so patiently it set her teeth on edge. "Let me get clear on this. You don't understand *anything*. Or wait. You *do* understand—everything, including the motivations of my ex-wife, a woman you've never met, a woman you know next to nothing about."

"Yes. Exactly. I know nothing about her. Nothing except what you've told me, and that isn't much. Because you don't *talk* to me—not about Belinda, not about anything that really matters to you."

"Cleo." He sounded more patient than ever now. A mature adult dealing with a thoroughly stubborn child. "What the hell is the problem here? What's the matter with you tonight?"

I'm having your baby and I don't even know *you, that's what's the matter.* "I want to feel…close to you. But I don't. Except when we're making love. That's what the problem is, that's what's bothering me."

He raked his hair back from his forehead, a gesture that clearly communicated how aggravated he was with her. "Look. I told you. I told you all of it. Belinda didn't like Atlantic City, she didn't like my line of work. She wanted me to move back to Bridgewater and get myself a nice, steady nine-to-five job. I wouldn't do that. She knew when we got married what I would do for a living. She said she accepted that that would be our life. And then, as soon as she married me, she started trying to change me. So maybe you ought to ask yourself, Cleo, is that what you're doing? Trying to change me?"

She replied softly, with certainty, "No."

He picked up his shoes, laid his jacket and shirt over his arm and swept to his feet. "Sure as hell seems like it to me." He started for the dressing room, his long strides swift.

She spoke to his back. "I don't want to change you, Fletcher. I just want to *know* you."

He stopped and turned to her, light eyes somber and full of shadows. "You know me as well as anyone does."

"Which is not very well at all."

His mouth was a thin line. "If you wanted some guy you could push around, you probably should have stuck with that damn mechanic."

That hurt. A lot. *Maybe I should have,* she thought. But she managed to hold the cruel words back. She didn't really feel that way. It would only have been anger talking, the sharp urge to wound him as he had just wounded her.

"I don't want a man to push around," she said carefully. "And just for the record, I never pushed Danny around. And you're right. I might have married him. He's a good man."

His lip curled in something very like a snarl. "You think I want to hear about how terrific your old boyfriend was?"

With effort she kept her voice even and calm. "You didn't let me finish. Danny *is* a good man. But he's not the man for me. *You* are, Fletcher. I love *you.* I truly do. I want to feel close to you. And I just don't."

He looked at her for the longest time, a bleak, closed-in sort of look. And then he turned and went into the dressing room, quietly shutting the door behind him.

Once he'd shut the door on his wife, Fletcher stripped off his slacks, his boxers and socks.

He took his sweet time about it. No need to hurry. There was nothing but trouble waiting back in the bedroom.

Yeah. He was mad.

It bugged him, just thinking about her old boyfriend. He never should have brought that subject up and he knew it. But now and then he did wonder....

Did she make comparisons? And when she did, was it Fletcher who came out the loser? She was always talking about openness, about trust and sharing. He'd only met the mechanic once, but he'd recognized him instantly as one of the nice guys, one of the guys women always say they can *talk* to.

Cleo claimed that she loved *him*. Fletcher believed in her love. He also believed she could love him and still wish she'd made a different choice.

He wondered if she imagined what it might have been like had she stayed with the mechanic, gotten herself a nice white-picket-fence kind of life with a husband who spilled his guts to her every night of the week, a husband who was always home for dinner and eager to tell her all about his *feelings,* a husband who *shared*.

Feelings, sharing, openness...

Lately he'd gotten so angry just hearing those words that it made him want to break something.

He wasn't a touchy-feely guy in the first place. And then there was the uncomfortable fact that she had it right.

Fletcher did have a secret—a secret he saw no percentage in *sharing*. Not with Cleo, not with anyone.

After he undressed, he carefully hung up all of his clothes, though he knew damn well he didn't have to, that Mrs. Dolby would take care of it all in the morning. He was stalling. He was making her wait. It was a petty way to behave and he knew it. But he did it anyway.

By the time he'd finally returned to the bedroom, Cleo had switched off her lamp and turned on her side, facing the wall, leaving the overhead recessed lights on low so he wouldn't be left completely in the dark.

She lay very still—too still—the blankets up tight around her neck. He knew damn well she wasn't sleeping.

He moved quietly to his side of the bed and looked down at her bundled shape beneath the covers. In spite of his fury with her, he admired the soft gleam of her hair in the faint light from above, the gentle inward curve of her waist, the tempting swell of her hip….

He felt his sex stirring. He wanted her. He always did. But this time, he knew, she wouldn't welcome his kisses. If he touched her, she'd only pull away—or insist on hashing things out some more. Neither possibility appealed to him. So he turned off the dim lights, slid under the blankets and kept his hands to himself.

He lay there, feeling her tight stillness beside him, aware of her careful, too-quiet breathing.

In time, her breathing grew more relaxed, more

shallow and even. She slept. But it wasn't an easy sleep. She made small, unhappy noises. She kept turning restlessly from her side to her back and then over to her side again.

Still wide-awake, Fletcher stared at the shadowed ceiling. Déjà vu all over again, as the old ballplayer once said. His second marriage was ending up way too much like his first.

Ending up...

Bad word choice.

His marriage to Cleo was not going to end. Cleo wasn't the least like Belinda. Cleo had a life of her own, a busy, successful career. And she'd been born and raised in Vegas. There was nowhere else she was dying to escape to.

And even if she did sometimes imagine a life without him, she would never leave Ashlyn. Cleo loved Ashlyn unconditionally and without reservation.

She was also incredible with Ashlyn. His daughter had been a damn good kid before Cleo came along. But the little sweetheart was downright amazing now. She called Cleo Mommy and she was happier, more outgoing, more sure of her place in the world.

Hell, *he* was happier with Cleo in his life. She made coming home the best part of the day.

And yeah, he knew he wasn't home enough. He'd promised her he would be. He would have to watch that, make a constant effort not to slip back into workdays that never seemed to end. Maybe that would do the trick, make it so she didn't feel the need to rag on him.

As to the other, to those questions about Belinda…

She would stop asking eventually. At heart, Cleo was a practical woman. She'd get the picture that demanding to know all his secrets was getting her nowhere—fast. She'd give it up and settle in to enjoy the good life they had together. She'd forget about Belinda. She'd stop hounding him for answers he was never going to give her.

Chapter Fifteen

One day faded into the next and Cleo failed to tell Fletcher that they were having a baby. The moment never seemed right—or so she told herself. But when six days had gone by and she still hadn't said the words, *I'm pregnant,* she began to realize that her silence had nothing to do with getting the timing right.

She was angry with him. And she was hurt at the way he'd hinted that she might still have romantic feelings for Danny. So she was getting even by not telling him about the baby.

Talk about self-defeating behavior. She felt he didn't share his heart with her—so she refused to share her news with him. Uh-uh. Bad approach. Not constructive in the least.

As a matter of fact, since the argument Tuesday night, they were hardly speaking. They were…achingly polite with each other. But nothing that mattered got said. At night, in bed, they would turn to each other and share lovemaking as passionate as ever.

But the rest of the time?

Strained would be the word for it.

Still, Fletcher did continue to make an effort to be around on the weekends, to get home by a reasonable hour. On the next Tuesday night, a week from the day she'd taken the home test, he called at six and promised he'd be in by eight.

She had Ashlyn fed and bathed and all ready for bed when Fletcher came in the door. The little girl ran to hug her father, and Cleo met Fletcher's eyes over the silky brown head of the child.

"Hi," he said softly.

She gave him a tremulous smile. "Hi."

Ashlyn pulled back enough to look at him. "I had a wonderful day, Daddy. At school, we are adding and taking away. And working with shapes. You know, triangles, squares, circles? We made foot butterflies. You put your feet together on paper and trace them and then make a butterfly from the shape. That was fun. And I am filling my word box, Daddy. I am filling it sooooo full." She stretched out her arms wide to indicate just how full. "Words are popping out all over." She laughed—a happy, musical laugh, a laugh that was new over the past few weeks. Then she hugged him hard again. "Oh, Daddy. I'm so glad you're home."

He planted a kiss on her velvety cheek. "And I'm glad to be home."

When he let her slide to her slippered feet, she grabbed his index finger. "C'mon. Let's go in the fam'ly room and you can—"

Cleo cleared her throat. When Ashlyn sent her an impatient sideways glance, Cleo shook her head.

The little girl let out a heavy sigh. "Oh, o-*kay*." She faced her father. "Mommy let me wait for you, but now I have to go to bed. You can take me."

"Lead the way." He cast another glance at Cleo.

She said, "I'll be in the family room."

He gave her a nod, and Ashlyn towed him off down the hall that led to her room, chattering away about her friends and her latest book as they went.

Ten minutes later he joined her.

On edge over the news she would soon be sharing with him, she jumped to her feet as he entered the room. "Are you hungry? I could—"

But he was already shaking his dark head. "I had a late lunch. I'm fine."

So she dropped to the couch again, folded her hands in her lap and stared blindly down at them. She'd promised herself she would tell him tonight. Absolutely.

Too bad she had no idea how to begin. Her gaze fell

on the latest issue of *NightLife* magazine. It lay before her on the coffee table. Her father's picture was on the front. She gestured at it. "Did you see this? I'm officially *outed* as Matthew Flint's love child."

"I heard. And yes, Marla made sure I had a copy on my desk, so I got a chance to read the interview this afternoon."

She shook her head. "I never thought I'd see the day. He *volunteered* the information, did you notice?"

Fletcher nodded. "Your father's proud of you. That's very clear. And he has every reason to be."

She warmed at his praise. "I, um, called him this morning, after I saw the article."

"Great."

"We had lunch. It was really nice." Things were working out beautifully with her father.

Too bad she couldn't say the same about her marriage. She cleared her throat and looked down at her hands again and didn't know what to say next.

The couch shifted as he sat beside her. "Hey."

"Hey." She made herself look up into his eyes. Did she see hope there, a desire that things might be better between them? She chose to think so. "Oh, Fletcher. I do want…for us to get along, you know?"

His gaze scanned her face. "I'm with you on that one."

"I'm sorry that we haven't been very, um, friendly with each other these last few days."

"I'm sorry, too."

She stared in his eyes and she believed that he *was* sorry. Not sorry enough to tell her what troubled him, but regretful that they'd shared harsh words, that they hadn't made up until now.

It wasn't the heart-deep closeness she couldn't stop longing for. But it was probably the best she would get from him.

He took her hand. And then he stood, pulling her up with him. He kissed her and she marveled as she always did at her own instant heated response to him.

When he raised his head, it was only to put one arm at her back and the other behind her knees and lift her high against his chest. She tucked her head into the curve of his shoulder and clasped her hands around his neck. He swept her off down the hall.

In their bedroom he undressed her slowly and made beautiful love to her. She responded eagerly to his every caress.

Later, lying close beneath the covers, they spoke of Ashlyn's upcoming two-week trip to see her grandparents in Bridgewater. Ashlyn was scheduled to leave that weekend. Cleo would fly out with her and return alone on Sunday, then repeat the same process when it was time for Ashlyn to come home.

"You don't really have to go with her," Fletcher said. "She'll have staff to look out for her every minute of the trip." They were taking one of the Bravo Group jets.

"But I want to go," she told him. "She's only five. And it's nicer for her to have a parent with her on a long flight like that."

He reached across to tip her chin his way. His smile was tender. "You're a hell of a mother, Cleo."

She made a soft noise in her throat. "Thank you."

The truth was she wanted to meet Belinda's parents. She hoped to get to know them a little. They were Ashlyn's grandparents after all. They might even shed some light on the mystery of Fletcher's relationship with their daughter.

He pulled her close once more. The slow, sweet loving began all over again.

And when the morning came, she still had yet to tell him that she was having his child.

Cleo and Ashlyn took off on Saturday at four in the morning. They arrived at Teterboro Airport a few minutes after twelve noon. Deanna and Jim Norton, both white-haired and well into their sixties, were there to meet them.

The Nortons lived in a rambling farm-style house set far back from the street, reached by a sweeping turn-around driveway shaded with well-established oaks and locust trees. Inside, the house was homey and inviting, with hardwood floors, clean white walls and comfy-looking floral-upholstered furniture. Pictures of Belinda lined the hallway that led to the bedrooms.

Cleo spent some time studying those photos of Fletcher's former wife. She saw Belinda as a fat little baby, naked on a yellow blanket after her bath. And as a little girl who looked much like her daughter, but with Jim's blue eyes and Deanna's slightly pointed jaw. There were pictures of Belinda with her parents, with girlfriends or perhaps cousins, a shot of her in a sundress out on the front lawn beneath the oaks, smiling shyly, her arm hooked in the arm of a young Fletcher—Belinda Norton, who became Belinda Bravo, a tall, pretty brunette with an engaging smile. She stood outside a brick building in a graduate's cap and gown. And in a church with a stained-glass window behind her, she was gloriously beautiful in a white wedding dress...

Deanna, who had a soft voice and a gentle smile, told Cleo they'd lived in the house for thirty-five years. Belinda had never known another home until she'd married Fletcher.

Late in the afternoon, when Ashlyn was napping and Jim had settled into his favorite recliner with a fat James Michener novel open on his lap, Deanna asked Cleo if she might enjoy a walk.

Outside, it was humid but not too hot. A slight breeze teased the oaks. The two women walked down the curving drive and along a well-maintained road from which driveways very much like the Nortons' curved away under the dappling shadows of the trees. Cleo, accustomed to the desert, marveled at the silky moistness of the air and the lush green growth all around them.

There were no sidewalks. A car rushed by a little too close for comfort, the air it stirred up ruffling Cleo's hair.

Deanna, on the inside, chuckled and took Cleo's arm. "Watch out. We can't have you run down, now can we?"

They moved a little farther onto the shoulder, but Deanna kept hold of Cleo's arm. It was nice, Cleo thought. Companionable. Strolling under the trees, a friendly arm hooked in hers.

Deanna said, "She laughs now, Ashlyn does."

"She's a joy."

"You're good for her."

Cleo glanced Deanna's way. They shared a look of perfect understanding before Cleo once again turned her gaze to the oak-shaded road ahead.

Deanna said, "The first time I heard her call you Mommy, well, I admit, that did hurt a little."

"It's natural that it would. But I promise, she'll never forget Belinda. I'll see to it."

"Thank you."

"And she'll be coming here regularly. You can show her the pictures in the hallway and talk of Belinda with her. Tell her your memories, make them *her* memories, too."

"Yes." Deanna's voice was soft as the spring breeze. "Yes, I'll do that."

"These days," Cleo said, "it's become an ordinary thing. Kids have mothers and stepmothers, both. They don't mind at all having two moms—or two dads, for that matter. They don't see it as any kind of contradiction. It's just…the way it is."

"Yes," said Deanna. "Yes, I see that." They strolled on in silence for a while. Then Deanna spoke again. "I was thirty-eight when I had Belinda. She was our only, as maybe you know. Our only and a late-in-life child. Jim was in real estate and making a success of it. He wasn't home much in those days. And I was…well, I wasn't a very good mother, I'm afraid. I spoiled Belinda rotten, gave her whatever she wanted. I felt a little over-whelmed with a first baby at that point in my life. But oh, did I love her. I hadn't realized how much I longed for a child until she came along. She was my miracle baby. I wanted above all for her to be happy and somehow I could just never manage to tell her no."

Cleo, well-versed in the ways of children, winced. "Disaster…"

Deanna's chuckle had a rueful sound. "That's the word. She grew up believing what I had taught her. That all she had to do was make a big enough fuss and even-tually she'd get things her way." Deanna shook her head. "So unfortunate. I do think that Fletcher's a fine man. But he's very busy with his work, isn't he?"

"Yes, he is."

"And Belinda always demanded a *lot* of attention. I suppose, looking back, that the two of them were pretty much destined *not* to make it. By the end of their marriage, she was here at home half the time, out late every night…."

Cleo put her hand over Deanna's, where it lay in the crook of her arm. "I'm sorry—not that that helps any. It's a great tragedy, to lose your child."

"It was…such a shock. So completely out of the blue. The truth is, my daughter was no better at being a mother than she'd been at being a wife. But she had a job she liked at a little boutique in town. She'd seemed…happier in those final months. More settled, less frantic somehow. And then, on a sunny Sunday afternoon, she went to take a nap…." Deanna was silent, collecting herself.

Cleo said softly, "I heard it was a stroke."

"Yes…"

Cleo squeezed the other woman's hand. "I understand that you took care of Ashlyn while Belinda was alive."

"I did."

"And you did a wonderful job with her. You know that, don't you?"

"Oh, I do hope so. It helps to believe that we've learned from the mistakes of the past."

The next morning at nine Cleo hugged Ashlyn goodbye.

"You come pick me up, Mommy," Ashlyn instructed.

"I'll be here. I promise."

"Come back anytime," Deanna told her, warmth and welcome in her eyes.

Jim nodded and echoed, "Anytime."

Cleo thanked them for their hospitality and boarded the jet for home, where Fletcher had a limo waiting to drive her to Impresario.

The apartment was empty. Mrs. Dolby had taken her Sunday off and Fletcher was working. He'd left her a note, propped up on the kitchen table: *Home by eight. F.*

She put her things away and then went down to her office at KinderWay and dealt with a stack of paperwork. At four, feeling slightly queasy and a little bit jet-lagged, she went back up to the penthouse and stretched out on the bed.

The queasy feeling quickly passed, but she wondered if she'd just had her first taste of morning sickness. She put her hand on her flat belly. So amazing, to think that she carried a tiny new life within her. She'd need to schedule an initial visit with an obstetrician—but who?

Celia would know. Cleo would call her tomorrow, find out who she was using.

A baby...

Now that would mean some changes in terms of her schedule at KinderWay. When the baby came, she'd have to cut back, at least for a while. It shouldn't be too terribly difficult. Megan, her associate director, was working out wonderfully. Megan would have no trouble filling in for Cleo wherever she was needed.

The phone by the bed rang. She reached over and picked it up. "'Lo."

"I'm guessing you got home safe." Fletcher.

Guilt jabbed at her. Here she lay, thinking of the baby and the steps she needed to take, the changes that would have to be made—and she had yet to let her husband in on the news that she was pregnant.

Then, as quickly she felt the stab of guilt, she ordered it away.

Why *should* she feel guilty? She hadn't told *anyone*.

When the time came that she wanted to talk about it, he'd be the first to know.

Her conscience whispered, *Celia will know tomorrow, when you ask her for a referral to her obstetrician....*

So fine, she'd wait a while on that.

"Cleo? You there?"

"Sorry. Yes. I'm here."

"Did the Nortons treat you right?"

"They did. I really liked them."

"Great. Was Ashlyn good for the trip?"

"As always."

"You sound tired."

"A little. I was just lying here thinking I might take a nap."

"Go for it. And I'll see you at eight. Be naked."

She laughed. He said goodbye. She put down the phone and curled up on her side. Her eyes drifted shut....

And she jolted wide-awake as the phone rang again. She grabbed it as it shrilled out for the second time.

"Hullo?"

"Well, hi." A woman's voice, rough and low and sexy. "I'm over at High Sierra, checkin' on Aaron—which, I don't mind telling you, he just hates for me to do—and I find myself wondering how you been gettin' along."

"Uh...Caitlin?"

"That's right. Meet me at Casa d'Oro, twenty minutes." Casa d'Oro was a High Sierra restaurant—midpriced, with Mexican and California cuisine. "We'll have us a pair of those *margaritas grandes*. I'll tell you about the current love of my life who is twenty-six and very frisky, and you can tell me how my sons' brother's been treating you."

The last thing Cleo wanted—or needed—was a margarita right then. And discussing Fletcher with Caitlin?

Bad idea.

Or was it? Caitlin might be a tad brash and rough around the edges, but the things she'd said on Cleo's wedding day still gave her pause every time she thought of them.

"Darlin', the silence is deafening. Don't tell me you're not dying for a giant margarita?"

"No, I'm not."

"Why? You pregnant or something?"

Cleo stifled a gasp. How could the woman have known?

The answer came: Caitlin *didn't* know. She'd only been teasing.

And Cleo had taken too damn long to figure that out.

Caitlin got the picture. Crystal clear. "You *are*. You're pregnant."

"I never said that."

Caitlin crowed. "No, you didn't. But that doesn't mean you're not."

Cleo pushed herself to a sitting position and raked her hair back out of her eyes. "Listen. Caitlin…"

"Darlin', settle down now. I been pregnant a time or two. I understand how it is. Sometimes a woman wants to keep it to herself for a while." Cleo swallowed a low noise of agreement. Just because Caitlin guessed the truth didn't mean Cleo had to confirm it. Caitlin went on, "I know I come across as someone with a very big mouth. You'd think I couldn't keep a secret to save my immortal soul. But I'm gonna surprise you. Nobody will hear the news from these lips of mine—and what d'you say we treat ourselves to a little change of subject about now?"

"Great idea."

"I still want to see you. If you don't want to come across the skyway, how 'bout I come on up to your place?"

"Uh…now?"

"Honey, your lack of enthusiasm is not reassuring. You're gonna hurt my feelings if you don't watch out."

Cleo couldn't help grinning. Really, Caitlin Bravo was one of a kind. "Sure. Come on over. I'm in the—"

"Say no more, sweetheart. I know where you live. I know where *everybody* lives."

Fifteen minutes later Caitlin was sitting on the sofa in the family room, wearing a red satin shirt, tight black jeans and tooled cowboy boots, enjoying a double whisky on the rocks.

She knocked back a big gulp, swallowed and grinned. "Now that really hits the spot, I gotta tell you." She arched a black eyebrow. "You really ought to have one of these—'less you're pregnant, of course…."

Cleo looked right at her—and didn't say a word.

"Awright, awright." Caitlin sipped some more and then launched into a long story about her boyfriend,

Lars. In the past decade or so, she confessed, she'd developed a definite preference for younger men. "And Scandinavians. Oh, my yes! Give me a sweet young guy from Norway or Sweden every damn time—so how's married life treating you?"

"Just great."

Caitlin ran her finger around the rim of her glass. "Smile when you say that."

"Caitlin, I swear, you are the nosiest person in all of Nevada."

The other woman laughed her deep, sexy laugh. "Guilty as charged. And I am picking up some extremely negative vibrations here."

Cleo looked away—and then back.

Caitlin urged more softly, "Come on. I meant what I said on the phone a while ago. I will keep whatever you tell me to myself." Still Cleo said nothing. Though she did want to. Badly. Caitlin sat forward, bracing her elbows on her knees and dangling her drink from her strong hands with their long bloodred fingernails. "Look. I'm a contented woman now. We had a rough road, my boys and me. But in the end they married good girls from the old hometown and they're happy, all three of 'em. Fletcher, though? Well, I love him like my own. How could I help it? He's so much like my boys. I knew the first time I met him that he wasn't happy. One look in his face and I could see that. Then he married you. I like you. I knew, like I said on your wedding day, that you're the one to get through to him." Caitlin shifted, sitting back and crossing her legs. "I'll tell you straight. Before I called you today, I went to see Celia."

Cleo stiffened. "What did she tell you?"

Caitlin was shaking that hard black head. "She told me nothing. She wouldn't go spillin' something you told her in confidence. Celia's not that kind. She was vague, that's all. Too vague. And she said you were fine. I'm fifty-eight years old. I know that 'fine,' as a general rule, means anything but." She leaned forward again. "He's shutting you out, isn't he?"

"No, he—"

"Uh-uh. Don't do that. Don't go lyin' to me."

Cleo glanced away. But when she looked back, Caitlin was still sitting there. Waiting. "Yeah," she confessed at last, accepting the fact that Caitlin knew already anyway. "I don't know how to get through to him. And I don't even really know...what it is that isn't right. I believe that he's true to me. He says he loves me. I believe that, too. He works too much, but I knew that he would when I married him. He does the best he can, I think."

"No, he doesn't. He's a brilliant man. He's got the brains and the heart to do better."

"Caitlin, how can you know that for sure?"

"I got a real sense for these things. And I know how it goes. It's the Bravo family way. A Bravo man can be difficult, especially if he's Blake Bravo's son. All of Blake's sons have his wild, troublesome blood running in their veins and they need a whole bunch of help from just the right woman in order to make themselves good, happy lives. The main thing is that you have to keep tryin', that you never give up. That you work at it, keep plugging away at him until he finally lets you in."

"I don't know. I've been thinking that what I really need to do is to learn to accept him for who he is."

Caitlin sniffed in utter disdain. "Stop. Wrong. Big mistake. You don't want to do that, you really don't."

"Oh, come on. Listen to what you just said. It's a *mistake* to let the poor man alone, to back the heck off, let him have his privacy and be grateful for what I've got?"

Caitlin's dark eyes glittered. "To settle. That's what you're saying in a roundabout way. And yeah, I think settling for a marriage that's not what you want your marriage to be is a major mistake, one you'll only keep regrettin', building bitterness on bitterness. In the end you'll be pushing *him* away, keeping your own secrets from him, shutting him out just like he does to you."

Cleo flat-out gaped. It was already happening. She was already doing exactly what Caitlin had just described, withholding the news of the baby from him, playing his game right back at him, keeping a secret of her own. "But…I can't change him. *He* has to do that. And he's made it pretty clear that he doesn't plan to change."

"Darlin', that's only because you haven't made it *necessary* for him to change."

"And how exactly am I supposed to make it necessary?" As Cleo asked that question, she realized how truly desperate she'd become.

Only pure desperation could bring her to ask Caitlin

Bravo's advice on this subject. Really, how much could Caitlin know about making a marriage work? Her only husband had been a notorious polygamist, kidnapper, murderer and all-around bad seed, a man who had disappeared from her life before her third son was even born.

Caitlin asked, "Where's the little one?"

"Ashlyn? She's at her grandparents' in New Jersey for a couple of weeks."

"Perfect."

"Excuse me?"

Caitlin leaned even closer and lowered her voice to a confidential whisper. "You need a break. You need to get the hell out of here."

"You mean…leave him?"

"Well, I wouldn't call it leaving him. Not permanently anyway."

"But I don't see how my leaving him—temporarily or otherwise—will solve anything."

Caitlin knocked back the rest of her drink and plunked the empty glass on the coffee table between them. "It's like the old song says, honey. How can he miss you if you won't go away?"

Chapter Sixteen

At eight-oh-two that night, Fletcher stood in the kitchen reading the note Cleo had left on the table next to the phone.

I'm safe. Don't worry about me. I need a little time to myself, that's all. Love, Cleo.

He yanked out a chair and dropped into it.

Then he read the damn note again. And again.

After ten times through, it still didn't make one iota of sense to him. If he hadn't recognized her handwriting, he'd have sworn that Cleo couldn't have written it.

She was safe—where? And for how long? And why the hell had she taken off in the first place? He'd talked to her not four hours ago and there had been zero mention of her taking off for some *time to herself.*

Uh-uh. This wasn't like her. Not in the least. Cleo was a mature and responsible woman. She didn't write notes like this. She didn't *do* crap like this. No. Something had to be wrong.

Then he got it. He understood.

His wife had been kidnapped. That had to be it. She'd never run off without telling him, not unless she had no choice.

God. Cleo. *Kidnapped.*

The thought sent his pulse into overdrive and made a coppery taste on his tongue. He couldn't sit still. Shooting to his feet, he grabbed the phone to call the police. Before he had a chance to punch up 911, the thing rang in his hand.

Hope spearing through him like a bolt of white-hot lightning, he punched the talk button and put it to his ear. "Cleo?"

"Hello, Fletcher."

Not Cleo. Some other woman. Was this the ransom call then? He growled into the phone, "Who's this?"

"It's Caitlin."

His adrenaline-juiced brain struggled to comprehend. "Caitlin. Bravo?"

"That's right."

Not the kidnapper after all. "Listen, Caitlin, I can't talk now." He yanked the phone from his ear to disconnect the call.

Just as he was about to push the off button, he heard her say, "Fletcher, you still there? I got a message for you from Cleo."

He put the phone to his ear again and demanded, "You what?"

"Cleo asked me to call you, to tell you that she really is safe like the note on the table says. She's where *she* wants to be and she'll be home. In her own good time. So don't worry, okay?"

He dropped into the chair again. "I don't get it. What in hell is going on?"

"Well now, Fletcher, there's a question for you. What in hell is going on that your wife who loves you would pick up and leave town out of nowhere like this?"

"Damn it, Caitlin. I want to talk to Cleo. Now."

"Bye, Fletcher."

"Wait! Damn you, don't you—" About then he heard the dial tone. She'd hung up on him.

Was this really happening?

He checked the display to call her back. Out of Area, it said. Wouldn't you know it? The bitch.

But wait. If Cleo hadn't been kidnapped after all, he should be able to reach her on her cell....

He tried it. Got the damn answering service and left a curt message.

"This is Fletcher. Call me." Then, with a series of very ugly words scrolling through his brain, he auto-dialed Aaron at his apartment.

Celia answered. "Bravo residence."

"It's Fletcher. I wonder if you've got a number for Caitlin."

"Sure." She sounded cheerful and relaxed. "At home? Her cell? Or at the Highgrade?"

"Give me all of them, whatever you've got." He rose again and foraged a pen and a scrap of paper from a drawer. "Ready."

She read them off and he scribbled them down. Then she asked, sounding more concerned than before, "Is something wrong? Why do you need Caitlin?"

It occurred to him that if Caitlin knew what the hell was up with Cleo, Celia probably did, too, however innocent her voice happened to sound.

"Cleo's gone." He said the words and couldn't believe they could possibly be true. But apparently they were. "You got any idea where she went?"

"What? Gone…where? Why?" She really did seem worried. And like Cleo, Celia was a straightforward type. He changed his mind. Evidently she *didn't* know.

He decided he'd better make a few reassuring noises. "Look. She's safe. She's fine. She left a note. And Caitlin just called me on a blocked line to tell me that Cleo told *her* that she really is okay."

"Caitlin's…involved?"

"It sure as hell looks that way."

"It's sometimes not so good when Caitlin's involved."

"Great to know, Celia."

"And wait a minute. You don't know where Cleo went?"

"No clue. I came home just now and there's this note on the table. A very short note. It says she's safe and she needs some time to herself."

A silence on the line, then she said, "Oh."

He wanted to strangle someone. Too bad there was no one nearby. He asked, very carefully, "What does that mean, 'oh'?"

"It means that the note sounds pretty clear to me."

"What do you mean, clear? She took off. Cleo wouldn't take off."

"Well, Fletcher, apparently that's just what she's done."

Fletcher tried Caitlin again. All three numbers. She wasn't at her restaurant/bar, the Highgrade. A waitress answered the phone. He left a curt message with her. Caitlin didn't pick up at her home number either or on her cell. He left messages at both of them. Angry ones.

And then he sat back down at the table and stared into space for a while, hoping that maybe Caitlin would check her messages and give him a call back.

Didn't happen.

He sat there some more, staring at the doorway to the hall, holding Cleo's note in his hand, kind of thinking that any minute now the front door would open and it would be Cleo, breezing in on those long, fine legs of hers, giving him a sweet, rueful smile, reassuring him that there was nothing to get freaked about. That that stupid note had been a foolish mistake.

But Caitlin didn't call. And Cleo didn't come.

After about a half an hour he decided that sitting there in his empty apartment waiting for something to happen was pointless. It wasn't as if he didn't have a raft of work he could be doing.

He got up, tossed the note in the trash and went back out the door.

It was 2:15 a.m. when Fletcher returned to the apartment. He let himself quietly in the front door and then he stood there in the foyer for a moment, ears straining for a sound, for something—anything—that would indicate she'd returned during his absence.

The place was dead quiet. He glanced at the narrow macassar ebony table to his left: no keys, no purse. The light overhead was on low, as he'd left it. Through the wide arch before him the living room lay in darkness, lit only by the glittering Las Vegas night beyond the floor-to-ceiling windows.

But none of that meant anything, not really. She could have come in, have gone on down the hall to their bedroom without turning on another light, without setting her keys or bag on the entry table as she so often did….

He turned and went down the hallway, glancing into the kitchen, the dining room, the family room, scanning each dark space as he passed it. The rooms gave him nothing. If she'd been in them since he left, he'd couldn't tell.

The door to the master suite stood open. No lights on in there. He knew then that it would be empty; he could *feel* it, that emptiness. He went inside anyway, into the silent darkness.

Beyond the sitting room their bed waited undisturbed, the bedspread rolled back and the covers turned down invitingly—but not by Cleo. Mrs. Dolby always turned down the bed. Apparently the housekeeper had returned from her Sunday off.

Fletcher crossed the room and picked up the phone by the bed. He entered the code to get messages on the house line. Nothing. Not from Cleo—and not from that damned Caitlin either.

Punching buttons furiously, he called all Caitlin's numbers again, one after the other. No luck. As before, he left angry messages at each number. Then he took off his clothes, showered and went to bed.

He couldn't sleep. He missed the warm, sleek body of his wife at his side, missed her soft sighs and teasing, low laughter, missed her gentle voice and the warm, arousing touch of her hand.

He missed *all* of her. A hell of a lot.

What was she up to? What was she trying to prove?

Monday, in the morning, he tried Cleo's cell again—and again no answer.

He still hadn't heard from Caitlin and he considered flying up to the charming little hamlet near Reno that she called home. But he knew there was no point. It might have been marginally satisfying to confront the woman face-to-face, but he was getting the picture that Caitlin had said all Caitlin planned to say—for now anyway.

And what about KinderWay? he wondered. Cleo would never just leave her business without telling them her plans.

He called her office at the original location and asked for her associate, Megan Helsberg.

"This is Megan."

"Hello, Megan. Fletcher Bravo here. Listen, Cleo had to take off for a few days. It was all pretty rushed. I just thought I should maybe check with you to make sure that she'd called you."

"Why, thank you, Mr.—"

"Fletcher."

"Fletcher then. And yes. I heard from Cleo yesterday."

Finally. He was getting somewhere. He schooled his voice to betray nothing beyond a casual interest. "Good enough then—and one more thing…"

"Certainly."

"Did she happen to leave you a number where she could be reached? I'm not getting through on her cell…."

"Well, I have the cell—and some emergency numbers for a family member."

He knew who that family member would be. "Caitlin Bravo, you mean?"

"Yes. Do you need those numbers?"

"No, thanks. I've got them." He said goodbye.

And after that he decided he was being a candy-ass fool. If Cleo wanted to play this kind of rotten game, so be it.

He was through trying to track her down. Let her come home when she was damn good and ready. He'd deal with her then.

He went to work at eight and he came home at two and he exerted all his considerable will to ignore the fact that his wife had disappeared from his home and his life as swiftly and easily as a dust devil speeds away in a whirling wind.

Tuesday, Celia called. She wanted to know how he was.

He said, "Fine," in a low, curt tone that clearly communicated he was absolutely furious and getting madder by the minute.

For a nervous count of five Celia said nothing. Then she told him she'd called Caitlin, but Caitlin would only say that Cleo was okay and doing exactly what she wanted to do.

Then Aaron's wife got down to what was really on her mind. She said that Cleo *had* been upset lately, that Cleo felt he was secretive, that he didn't share what was going on inside him.

As if that was news. Far from it. It was only all the "trust, truth and sharing" stuff that he'd already heard—repeatedly—from the woman herself. "Anything else?"

"I just thought, well, you might want to know, that's all...."

He reminded himself that Aaron's wife was only trying to help. In a gentler tone he thanked her and said goodbye.

Somehow, in a fog of work and denial, he got through

Tuesday. He went to bed at three Wednesday morning, faded into an edgy sleep—and sat bolt-upright in bed an hour later.

"The mechanic," he growled into the darkness before dawn. And then he threw back the blankets.

Buck-naked in his study, he booted up the computer. He brought up the file on Cleo that Brian Klimas had prepared for him back in January, the one with the goods on Danny Pope: his background, his auto-restoration business, home address, work address, various phone numbers.

He printed the page. And then he went back to the bedroom and put on some chinos and a shirt.

Five minutes later he was in the elevator, on his way down to his private parking space and the Jag that he kept there.

Danny Pope had an ordinary house—pink stucco, tile roof—on an ordinary street not too far from the house that Cleo had recently sold. The first thing Fletcher noticed when he nudged the Jaguar in at the curb was that Cleo's SUV, gone from her parking space back at Impresario, was nowhere in sight here either.

Which didn't mean a damn thing. The mechanic had a two-car garage. Cleo's car could be in there, nuzzled up nice and cozy against Danny Pope's cherried-out classic Chevy Bel-Air.

Fletcher shut off the lights and the engine and then just sat there. What in hell was he doing? He was supposed to be finished with garbage like this. It was why he'd chosen Cleo; he knew she'd never pull any low-down stunts on him, that she was a straight shooter who would never betray her man.

Or at least, it was why he'd *told* himself he'd chosen Cleo.

The real reason was a hell of a lot more dangerous. The real reason was what had him sitting outside the mechanic's house in the darkest hour right before dawn, wondering what the hell he was doing here and telling himself he ought to start up the Jag again and get the hell out before he made a damn fool of himself.

Déjà vu, all right. Right back where he'd promised himself he would never be again….

And whatever he *ought* to do, he knew what he *had* to do. He *had* to know if Cleo was in that ordinary stucco house with the boyfriend she'd supposedly left behind—for him.

He leaned on the door and got out of the car. As he strode up the front walk he almost turned around twice—but not quite.

The porch was an alcove lit by the soft golden gleam of a lantern-style fixture mounted on the wall above the address plaque. He punched the bell and heard the chime echo through the rooms beyond the door.

He felt calm by then. A deadly sort of stillness was in him. He waited for several minutes, his veins full of ice, his patience without limit. If he had to wait on this porch forever, he would do it. He wasn't leaving without answers, no matter how rough the answers were.

Finally the door swung back and Danny Pope stood there in a brown-striped seersucker robe, eyes bleary, hair scrambled from sleep, hairy legs stuck into a beat-up old pair of mocs.

Pope squinted at him. "Uh…hey. Fletcher. How you doin'?"

"Not so great, Danny. I'd like to talk to my wife."

Danny squinted harder. "Huh? Cleo? I haven't seen Cleo in—"

Fletcher didn't want to hear it. He stepped over the threshold, sticking an arm out at the same time, shoving the mechanic out of the way and heading down the hall that branched out to the left.

"Hey! What the hell?" Danny fell against the wall with a heavy thud, scrambled to get his balance and then came barreling after Fletcher. "Man, hold up. You're way outta line…."

Fletcher ignored him. He peered into empty rooms as he went by them: a bathroom, a small bedroom. At the end of the hall a door stood open. From in there a woman called, "Danny? What's all that noise? What's goin' on?"

Fletcher froze in midstride. He spun to face the mechanic, who looked confused as hell and pretty teed off, too. "That's not Cleo."

The mechanic slowly shook his head.

"Danny?" the woman called again, slightly frantic now.

The mechanic edged around Fletcher and went to the open door. "It's all right, Sylvia, honey. An old buddy dropped by is all."

"You coming back to bed, hon?" Her voice was softer now, without the worried edge. Fletcher could hear a yawn in it.

"In a little bit." Quietly Danny shut the door. He scratched his head, then scrubbed his fingers back through his thatch of uncombed hair. He sent Fletcher a sideways look. "So," he said after a moment's thought. "How 'bout a beer?"

They ended up at the kitchen table with a couple of Budweisers in front of them.

Danny wanted to know what was going on. After barging into the man's house at five in the morning, Fletcher figured he owed the guy an explanation.

The strange thing was, once he started talking, he ended up telling his former rival considerably more than the other guy needed to know about Cleo, including the problems the two of them were having and the way she'd vanished on him three days before.

When he finished, Danny took a pull of his beer, swallowed thoughtfully and then advised, "The way I remember it, Cleo demands lots of communication from her man. You want to keep her, you better start talkin', if you know what I mean."

Fletcher swore and knocked back a slug of his own

beer. "I talk," he muttered. It sounded damned defensive even to his own ears.

Danny snorted. "It's pretty clear to me you don't talk *enough*. Or if you do, you don't talk about the things your wife needs to hear."

"Such as?" Fletcher grumbled.

"Hell, man. Only *you* know what you're keepin' from her." He braced a beefy forearm on the table and leaned on it. "I can tell you this much…."

"Go for it."

"Cleo's long-gone in love with you. No doubt about it. I got that message loud and clear the one and only time I saw you two together. You got her heart, you can take my word on that. But Cleo's a woman who won't settle for less than all a man's got." Danny tipped his beer bottle at Fletcher, pointing with it. "My advice is you'd better get wise and give her what she needs or eventually you *will* lose her."

"But where the hell is she? How can I *open up* to her if she's not here, damn it?"

"She'll be back," Danny predicted. "Soon. This runnin' away, it's not her style. In a day or two, tops, she'll be walking through your door again. And when she does…"

"What?"

"Start talkin', buddy. Don't blow it this time."

Fletcher got back to Impresario at six-thirty. When he let himself in the apartment, hazy morning light filled the living room beyond the foyer. He stared out at the misty daylight and thought, *Another day without her...*

He turned to toss his keys on the entry table.

And from behind him Cleo said softly, "Good morning."

Chapter Seventeen

Cleo stood in the arch to the main hallway. She wore an-kle-length black pants and a bright pink shirt. No shoes. He stared at her long bare feet with their pink-painted toenails and then slowly, not quite daring to believe, he let his gaze track up the gorgeous length of her.

Until he was looking right into those wonderful amber eyes. He wanted only to close the distance between them and grab her close in his aching arms. But he didn't.

He stayed where he was and asked quietly, "Did you have a safe trip—wherever the hell it was that you went?"

She caught her full lower lip between her white teeth, worried it a moment, then let it go. "Caitlin has this old house up in the mountains between Reno and Tahoe. It belonged to her mother. Nobody lives there, but Jilly and Will like to go there at Christmas, I think. It's quiet. Isolated. Nestled in the pines."

"And when you got there you...?"

She lifted one shoulder in a half shrug. "I took a lot of long walks. I read. I did some thinking...." He could have asked, *Thinking about what?* But he didn't. No need to. He already knew what she'd been thinking about: the two of them, their marriage that wasn't quite all she wanted it to be. She added, "It gets very lonely up there at night. I had some trouble sleeping. Haunted by sad dreams, I guess. There's no TV and no telephone...."

"No cell phone reception?"

"Intermittent at best." She looked down at her feet, then at him again. He watched as she pulled those graceful shoulders back, drawing herself up tall and straight. "I got your messages, though."

But you never bothered to call me back, did you?

He thought the question but didn't say it. They both knew she'd chosen not to return his calls. "When did you get here?"

"About an hour ago." Ironic. She'd returned not long after he'd left for Danny Pope's place. Sometimes life was just too damn much about timing.

Fletcher gazed at his wife, drinking in the sight of her: those worried eyes, that cinnamon hair, the soft mouth—all of her. Every glorious inch.

In terms of timing, this was one of those moments. He could see her love for him in those brandy-colored eyes, see the tension in her body, the yearning toward him—*and* the stark fear that they had lost each other, that what was wrong between them simply couldn't be made right.

He saw all those things and he understood them completely—after all, he felt them, too.

He took a step toward her and she took one toward him. "Thank God," he said, finally letting all his hope and yearning show. "You're…home." His voice broke on that last word *home.*

And he found himself thinking that *she* was his home. That with her, he had his chance at last to know a real, abiding love—and to return love in kind. To be the man his evil, lost daddy could never have been.

Her sweet mouth quivered. "Oh, Fletcher…"

And with a soft cry she was running toward him. She launched herself into his arms.

And he caught her, caught the slim, solid weight of her. He held her hard and close, buried his face in her sweet-smelling hair, whispered, "Cleo, I love you. Always. I do…."

"Oh, yes. I know. I love you, too."

He let her go—but only long enough to cup her glowing face in his cherishing hands. He kissed her.

It was heaven, that kiss.

His own heaven. Right here on earth.

When he lifted his mouth from hers, she smiled at him. A smile that made the morning all the brighter.

He said, "I went to Danny Pope's."

She frowned. "When?"

"Just now. I thought maybe…" He couldn't quite say it.

And then he found he didn't need to. Because she understood. "Oh, Fletcher. No. I would never do something like that. Never go to another man. Not in this life or the next. I love *you* and I belong with you."

He nodded. "I should have known. I *did* know. It's only…" He couldn't say the word.

So she said it for him. "Belinda." He hung his head. She touched his face, urged him to look at her. When he did, she said, "Belinda betrayed you, didn't she?"

He swallowed. "Yeah. Often. With a lot of different men."

She touched his face. "Oh, my darling. I'm so sorry…."

He turned his head enough to brush a kiss in the heart of her palm. Then he caught her hand. "I have more to say."

"Oh, I'm so glad."

She let him lead her down the hall, to the master suite. Once inside, he shut the door. They took seats on the sofa in the sitting area.

Holding tightly to her soft hand, he confessed, "Belinda was always fragile emotionally. She needed so much attention. And I was busy working. At first, there were scenes. She'd cry and complain that I never had time for her. Then she started sleeping around—one-night stands, all of them, as far as I know. The first few times she went to bed with other men, she threw the

news in my face. We fought. We made up. I…couldn't
leave her. I felt responsible for her."

"Well, of course you did. That's how you are. She
was your wife and that made her family and that meant
you had to stick by her."

He felt the wry smile as it pulled at his mouth. "Got
me all figured out, huh?"

"Well, I'm working on it."

"Never stop." He kissed her hand again.

"I don't intend to—and please, tell me the rest."

"Yeah." His throat clutched up on him again. He swallowed. And he went on, "After the first time she hooked
up with someone else, I…well, I didn't leave her. But I
couldn't touch her. And that only made her worse."

Cleo was nodding. "There were a few things Deanna
said last Saturday, about how Belinda was so demanding, how she would stay out all night…."

"Yeah. I think Deanna and Jim might have known
about her, about her thing for picking up strangers—
at least, they might have known subconsciously. But
they never talked about it. And it seemed so wrong to
bring it up to them, to tell them that their daughter was
pretty much screwing anything that moved. I didn't
say a word to them. And Belinda and I drifted further
and further apart. Now and then we'd try to reconcile,
to make it work between us. I even slept with her
once, near the end. I was depressed. I'd had a few
whiskies. The plain truth is, I wanted to get laid. I
wanted it bad."

Cleo's eyes glittered with unshed tears. "You were true to her, though she wasn't to you."

He smiled again, even more ruefully than before. "You make me sound so damn noble."

"Well, you were."

"Uh-uh. Not noble. Stubborn. Determined not to be like my bad daddy, determined to honor my wedding vows no matter what. Set on proving I wasn't in any way a chip off the old block. That's all."

Cleo sat back from him then. He saw in those soft eyes that she was putting it together. She brought a hand to her mouth, her eyes going wide. "Ashlyn," she said on a breath.

"Yeah."

"She's not…?"

"I don't know. She could be mine. There *was* that one time, and it was the *right* time for me to be Ashlyn's father. But Belinda said no. She threw it in my face the night she asked for a divorce. She screamed at me that the baby she was carrying *wasn't* mine. She said there had been a lot of men—so many, in fact, that she had no idea herself who the baby's father was."

"And that did it. You gave her what she wanted. A divorce, full custody…"

"That's right. And if she hadn't died suddenly, I would have never set eyes on Ashlyn. I would have sent the checks for her support and stayed the hell away from her. But then Belinda did die. And Deanna called me. And, well…I've always liked Deanna and Jim. I went back there, to Bridgewater, for their sakes. And I met Ashlyn. I'll never forget my first sight of her. She was wearing a pretty blue dress, sitting on the sofa in Deanna's living room. She looked up when I came in. Damn. Those incredible serious eyes of hers. She asked, 'Are you my daddy?' Hell. What else could I say?"

"Oh, Fletcher. Only what you did say. *Yes*."

The tears were trailing down her soft cheeks by then. He grabbed a tissue from the box on the low table beside them and handed it to her. She blew her nose and dried her eyes.

He said, "I've never told anyone else but you. And I never will. But I still don't know for sure if she's mine—if she's not. I had Klimas look into it without explaining why. He couldn't find any guy Belinda saw regularly. And yeah, I know there's the option of a paternity test. That would settle it. I'd know for certain."

She sniffed. "Oh, no…"

"Oh, no what?"

She tossed the tissue on the table and grabbed his hand again. "Listen. Are you listening?"

Even with a red nose and puffy eyes she was the most beautiful woman he'd ever seen. "Yeah. I hear you. Every word."

"Good. Because there's no need for any test. You *are* Ashlyn's father. In all the ways that matter, she is and always will be your daughter. And for now, well, there's not another thing to be done on that issue. Except to love her and take care of her."

"But maybe someday she'll—"

"Shhh." She leaned close, kissed him lightly into silence. "Listen to what you just said. *Someday.* Let's deal with someday when it comes along. For right now, you're all the father that little girl needs."

He tightened his hold on her hand. "There's more."

She squeezed back. "Tell me. Everything."

"Remember the morning I asked you to marry me?"

"How could I ever forget?"

"I didn't know, didn't realize until that morning, when you asked if I loved you and I said I did…I didn't know until I said the words that they were true. I loved you completely and I knew that I always would."

She almost smiled. "And that's a problem?"

"Yeah. For me, it was. Until then, I'd been telling myself that my decision to make you my wife was purely practical—and sexual. You were great with Ashlyn. She adored you. You knew my world, had lived in it. You understood how things work. Plus, I couldn't keep my hands off your gorgeous body. I told myself it was perfect. Not love, just an excellent match. But then you asked me if I loved you. I said I did—and it hit me. A knockout punch. I was telling the truth. I *did* love you. I wanted to marry you because I wanted to be with you for the rest of my life, and all my other trumped-up reasons were just so much crap. That scared me. You have no damn idea how much. I've been running from that—from how much I love you—ever since then."

"Oh, Fletcher…"

"Yeah?"

"You don't have to run anymore."

"Good. The bald truth is, running's just not working. No matter how damn hard I try, I can't escape the fact that I'm even more scared of losing you than I am of the power in what I feel for you. So if you'll give me a chance, I'll…work with it. I'll learn to accept that I'm hopelessly yours."

She laughed then. "Fletcher, you make it sound like a death sentence."

"No. A *life* sentence. That's what it is. You. Me. Forever…you think?"

"I don't *think*. I know."

"Good," he said, drawing her closer.

She sighed and pressed up against him, soft and so willing. He kissed her, a long, sweet kiss, a kiss as deep as his love for her.

When he lifted his head, it was only to settle her into the crook of his arm. For a moment they were quiet, sitting there on the sofa in the morning light. Together.

Then shyly she took his hand again and pressed it to her flat belly. "I've been keeping a secret, too." She tipped her head back, her gaze seeking his.

He dared to guess. "A baby?"

Her eyes were shining. "Yes."

And with that, at last, all the secrets had been told. He rose from the sofa and took her to their bed. They undressed each other slowly by the light of the morning sun.

And when he guided her down onto the pillows, he whispered, "I love you."

"And I love you."

"Forever."

She lifted her slim arms to pull him close. "Oh, absolutely. Forever and always. I wouldn't settle for anything less."

* * * * *

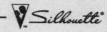
Silhouette®

SPECIAL EDITION™

PRESENTING A NEW MINISERIES BY

RaeANNE THAYNE:

The Cowboys of Cold Creek

BEGINNING WITH

LIGHT THE STARS
April 2006

Widowed rancher Wade Dalton relied
on his mother's help to raise three small
children—until she eloped with "life coach"
Caroline Montgomery's grifter father! Feeling
guilty, Caroline put her Light the Stars
coaching business on hold to help the angry
cowboy...and soon lit a fire in his heart.

DON'T MISS THESE ADDITIONAL BOOKS IN THE SERIES:

DANCING IN THE MOONLIGHT, May 2006
DALTON'S UNDOING, June 2006

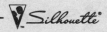
Silhouette®

SPECIAL EDITION™

DON'T MISS THE FIRST BOOK IN

PATRICIA McLINN's

EXCITING NEW SERIES

Seasons in a Small Town

WHAT ARE FRIENDS FOR?

April 2006

When tech mogul Zeke Zeekowsky
returned for his hometown's Lilac Festival,
the former outsider expected a hero's
welcome. Instead, his high school fling,
policewoman Darcie Barrett, mistook him
for a wanted man and handcuffed him!
But the software king and the small-town
girl were quick to make up....

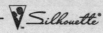

SPECIAL EDITION™

THE THIRD STORY IN

The MOOREHOUSE Legacy

A family tested by circumstance, strengthened by love.

FROM THE FIRST
April 2006

Alex Moorehouse had loved Cassandra Cutler from the first. Then she'd been his best friend's wife. Now she was a widow, which, for Alex, didn't change anything. Cassandra was still off-limits. And he was still a man who loved no one but her.

A 4–1/2–star Top Pick!
"A romance of rare depth, humor and sensuality."

—*Romantic times BOOKclub* on BEAUTY AND THE BLACK SHEEP, the first in *the Moorehouse Legacy*

If you enjoyed what you just read,
then we've got an offer you can't resist!

Take 2 bestselling love stories FREE!

Plus get a FREE surprise gift!

Clip this page and mail it to Silhouette Reader Service™

IN U.S.A.	IN CANADA
3010 Walden Ave.	P.O. Box 609
P.O. Box 1867	Fort Erie, Ontario
Buffalo, N.Y. 14240-1867	L2A 5X3

YES! Please send me 2 free Silhouette Special Edition® novels and my free surprise gift. After receiving them, if I don't wish to receive anymore, I can return the shipping statement marked cancel. If I don't cancel, I will receive 6 brand-new novels every month, before they're available in stores! In the U.S.A., bill me at the bargain price of $4.24 plus 25¢ shipping and handling per book and applicable sales tax, if any*. In Canada, bill me at the bargain price of $4.99 plus 25¢ shipping and handling per book and applicable taxes**. That's the complete price and a savings of at least 10% off the cover prices—what a great deal! I understand that accepting the 2 free books and gift places me under no obligation ever to buy any books. I can always return a shipment and cancel at any time. Even if I never buy another book from Silhouette, the 2 free books and gift are mine to keep forever.

235 SDN DZ9D
335 SDN DZ9E

Name	(PLEASE PRINT)	
Address	Apt.#	
City	State/Prov.	Zip/Postal Code

Not valid to current Silhouette Special Edition® subscribers.

Want to try two free books from another series?
Call 1-800-873-8635 or visit www.morefreebooks.com.

* Terms and prices subject to change without notice. Sales tax applicable in N.Y.
** Canadian residents will be charged applicable provincial taxes and GST. All orders subject to approval. Offer limited to one per household.
® are registered trademarks owned and used by the trademark owner and or its licensee.

SPED04R

©2004 Harlequin Enterprises Limited

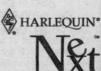

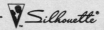

SPECIAL EDITION™

RETURN TO HART VALLEY IN

HER BABY'S HERO

BY

KAREN SANDLER

Elementary school teacher Ashley Rand
was having CEO Jason Kerrigan's baby.
Even though they came from different
worlds, each was running from trouble.
So when Jason rented the Victorian house
of Ashley's dreams, they both believed life
would slow down. Until they found out
Ashley was having twins!

Available April 2006
at your favorite retail outlet.

COMING NEXT MONTH